"JOHN SPARTAN,
SMITHERS, HIS VOI
ICY CHAMBER.

"You have been sentenced to seventy years sub-zero rehabilitation in the California Cryo Penitentiary. Your crime is the involuntary manslaughter of thirty –"

"Skip it," Spartan ordered.

The last thing he needed to hear before voyaging into eternity was a recitation of his crime – even if it had been a horrible mistake. He would maintain his innocence even if he was forced to take it with him to his frozen grave.

He was beginning to shake with the cold now, great racking shudders, chemical-induced tremors that shook his whole body. The blood in his face had drained away, leaving his skin a severe parchment white, the only colour in his face the burning intensity of his dark eyes and the ice-blue of his lips.

Spartan – no surprise – was not performing like the other men who had shared his horrible fate. They had screamed and twisted on their cold, subterranean gallows, desperately trying to break free. Spartan fought the process too, but not with his body – it was too late for that, a futile waste of energy. Spartan resisted with his mind ...

DEMOLITION MAN

A novel by Richard Osborne based on a story by Peter M. Lenkov and Robert Reneau and a screenplay by Daniel Waters and Robert Reneau and Peter M. Lenkov

A SIGNET BOOK

SIGNET

Published by the Penguin Group
Penguin Books Ltd, 27 Wrights Lane, London W8 5TZ, England
Penguin Books USA Inc., 375 Hudson Street, New York, New York 10014, USA
Penguin Books Australia Ltd, Ringwood, Victoria, Australia
Penguin Books Canada Ltd, 10 Alcorn Avenue, Toronto, Ontario,
Canada M4V 3B2
Penguin Books (NZ) Ltd, 182–190 Wairau Road, Auckland 10, New Zealand

Penguin Books Ltd, Registered Offices: Harmondsworth, Middlesex, England

First published in the USA by Signet, an imprint of Dutton Signet, a division of Penguin
Books USA Inc. 1993
Published in Great Britain 1993
1 3 5 7 9 10 8 6 4 2

Printed in England by Clays Ltd, St Ives plc

Like signs of doom written on the sky, vast clouds of thick black smoke lay low and threatening, funneled into the atmosphere from the angry orange flames of the burning city.

The city of Los Angeles was out of control.

The famous riot of 1992 was followed three years later, in the hot, murderous summer of 1995, by a bigger, more violent urban rebellion. The first riot lasted for just three days. The second would burn furiously for three weeks. Whole sections of the city were destroyed, hundreds of buildings left ruined, and thousands of people lost their lives.

The National Guard had not been force enough to restore order. By the time it was over, troops of the regular army, marines, and air force would be called in to reconquer the streets and control the skies.

In the city that was home to the movie industry—an industry addicted to the making of sequels—the riot of 1995 acquired a set of Roman numerals. It became known as Riot II.

In the months that followed, the Los Angeles Police Department ceased to be a peace-keeping agency and became instead a paramilitary force, an urban army larger and better armed than that of some sovereign nations. It was no surprise, then, that the next disturbance, in the summer of 1996, was more than a riot—it was a civil war.

Whole sections of the city became the private fiefdoms of war lords and their followers. The richer sections of the city were armed camps. The police no longer patrolled—they mounted campaigns; criminals did not commit crimes—they launched counteroffensives.

The conflict started in July of that year, and it had been going on ever since. Despite the intensity of the hostility, the strife came to be known by an old-fashioned name, nostalgia for a more conventional chaos. Everyone called it Riot III.

Helicopters beat through the dark sky, agile attack craft, thrashing above the riot-torn city, spewing tracer fire at nothing in particular on the ground. The thousands of heavy rounds were meant to pin down and isolate the marauders in the burning sections of downtown—containment action, the LAPD called it.

Once the attack squads had done their work, the specialists made their move, zeroing in on the latest and most serious hot spot requiring their unique and lethal skills.

The specialists traveled in style, roaring through the smoke-streaked sky in a heavily armed chopper, the biggest, blackest machine in the LAPD air force—a modified Sikorsky Blackhawk UH 60.

The helicopter was armed with 2 GE .50-caliber machine guns and wing pods carrying sixteen Hellfire missiles, not to mention a set of self-defense Stinger missiles to counter any really serious threat from the ground. More primitive dangers—mere bullets—were taken into account, too. The underside of the mammoth machine was heavily armored with thick sets of Kevlar matting, as if the belly of the machine was encased in a giant bulletproof vest.

The Blackhawk carried no registration numbers, no insignia, except for four gold letters on the black steel skin: LAPD. Two sets of powerful rotors hammered the air, driving the machine fast, as if the crew couldn't wait to find themselves in harm's way.

They didn't have to wait too long. A long rip of bullets fired from the ground tore along the undercarriage and spattered themselves flat against the steel plating on the port side.

Lieutenant Zachary Lamb, the pilot, and Schmidt, his copilot, reacted to the sudden attack, jinking the heavy machine to port and gaining a hundred feet.

Lamb shook his head. "Remember when they used to let commercial airliners land in this town? Never again! You can bet on that."

Schmidt nodded. "Yeah. The good old days—and they're gone for good."

A gunman on the roof of an abandoned office tower fired a half clip of 9-millimeter rounds at the passing aircraft—it was nothing personal, and he had nothing to gain by downing the chopper. He fired at it because it was there.

The bullets rattled along the side of the Blackhawk, and Schmidt immediately scoped the gunman on his look-down video screen.

"You want to have a chat with that guy?" His gloved hands felt for the triggers of the right side 7.62 M60s.

Lamb shook his head. "Naww. He didn't mean it—you could tell his heart wasn't in it. What's the point?"

"I don't understand where we're going and why the hell we're bothering anyhow . . ."

"Paycheck?" suggested Lamb.

A third person joined them on the flight deck.

"You're doing a good deed," said John Spartan. He was a tall, compactly muscled man, dressed in a black body suit overlain with a leather flack jacket, every pocket stuffed with equipment. Sewn into the collar of his vest was a small microphone that kept him in radio contact with the Los Angeles Police Department communications net.

"Maybe you got a better reason than that, Spartan. One that makes a little more sense."

"A maniac hijacked thirty people off a municipal bus," said Spartan. "How's that? I think that's a pretty good reason. Don't you?"

If Lieutenant Lamb had his doubts about Spartan's reason for the coming mission, he didn't let on. Instead, he just jerked a gloved hand at the porthole.

"You looked at the neighborhood, Chief? Nasty."

Spartan peered down at the maelstrom of fire and smoke that burned in the ravaged city and nodded to himself. "I've got a real bad hunch about who the maniac is and where the hostages are being held."

"You want to share it with us, Spartan?" asked Lamb. Like most pilots he had an aversion to flying blind. He always liked to know where he was going and why.

In this case, however, it was not a where or a why that had sent his heavily armed chopper aloft. It was a who.

"I'm looking for Phoenix," said Spartan. "Simon Phoenix."

In this case, Lamb realized that ignorance might have been better for his state of mind. He settled down in his seat and hunched over the controls, as if to make himself a smaller, less vulnerable target.

"I really might have been happier if I didn't know that," he grumbled.

"Oh man," groaned Schmidt, peering through the forward screen. "There it is."

Way up ahead, all three men could see that they were closing fast on a single square city block—a block that appeared to be in flames. Rising from the fiery center was a fortress, a walled enclosure that looked like something out of the Middle Ages, a bastion constructed from the refuse of the late twentieth-century American city: a sturdy brick warehouse girded in steel and encircled by a high wall made by the carcasses of abandoned cars piled fifty feet high.

Spartan gazed at the stronghold for a long moment, then moved to the back of the chopper, pushing back the sliding door on the side of craft and thrusting his head out into the slipstream of hot, smoky air. He looked downward for a moment, examining the terrain and judging the altitude, then stepped back into the payload of the aircraft and strapped himself into a harness.

Schmidt turned in his seat. "Hey, Spartan!"

The big cop was muscling a heavy canvas bag toward the open door. "What?"

"How come they call you Demolition Man?" He flashed a grin at Spartan. "Are you with the bomb squad or what?"

Spartan was too busy to give any kind of answer to that question. Lieutenant Lamb responded for his friend.

"He just . . ." Lamb shrugged. "Spartan just demolishes things."

John Spartan was set by the door now, gear and harness at the ready. He was in position, but the chopper wasn't, allowing him a more detailed answer to Schmidt's question.

"I do my job," he said, leaning into the cockpit. "Shit happens . . . Get me a thermo, will ya?"

The pilot punched a few buttons on the console in front of him, and the heat-sensitive cameras mounted in the nose of the helicopter scanned the fortress. The video scopes were sophisticated enough to filter out the peripheral heat of the fiery building and zoned in on the interior of the structure.

In a matter of seconds a schematic of the whole

building filtered up onto the liquid crystal display screen in the center of the cabin instrument panel.

"Remember, John," Lamb cautioned, "we're just sightseeing. That's all."

Spartan just grunted and stared at the thermo scene on the screen.

The radio crackled into life. "Tactical Hover Command One! Tactical Hover Command One! Come in. You are definitely in unauthorized air space, guys."

All three men ignored the warnings from the communication center at the LAPD air base. Schmidt concentrated on flying the craft, while Lamb and Spartan studied the thermal layout of the fortress.

"I register movement on . . . four, five . . . seven people," said Lamb. "There's no way there's thirty people in that building, Spartan. No way. Six on the perimeter, one in the middle. No hostages. No problem. Let's go home."

There was a note of relief in Lieutenant Lamb's voice, and he hoped that Spartan could hear it—and agree that it wasn't worth risking three necks to bag a handful of hard cases in a building no one really gave a damn about anyway.

Spartan wasn't so convinced. He tapped an area in the lower part of the screen. "Enhance that, would you? Can you get a read on it?"

To the naked eye there was nothing there. A pile of broken-down machinery, the rusting corpses of old cars covered by a large dirty tarp.

But the thermal eye saw through the debris, picking up the warm engine, drive train, and exhaust system of a sixty-foot municipal bus hastily hidden in the tangle of rubble. Spartan could even make out faint outlines of the bus's seats and frame.

"There it is," he said grimly. "That's the bus. And if the bus has been stashed here . . ." Neither Lamb nor Schmidt needed to hear the end of Spartan's deductive reasoning.

"Oh boy," moaned Schmidt.

John Spartan took a deep breath and worked his arms above his head, loosening his shoulders, first the left, then the right. Then he checked the guns on his hips—first the left, then the right, two heavy Ruger Redhawk handguns, both modified to carry sixteen-shot clips. If he went for them both at once, he could cross draw them with lightning speed and put thirty-two slugs in a target in a split second.

A voice from the radio console filled the flight deck. "Spartan, this is Healy. We've tracked your movements, and the LAPD is forbidding you to make a move. You are not to do one thing that might endanger those passengers."

Spartan glanced forward at the fortress, an ugly inferno. It seemed to him that the passengers had already been endangered—if they were still alive, that is.

The voice on the radio—Commander Healy, head of the Los Angeles Police Department Tactical Wing and Spartan's superior officer—was growing angrier.

"Spartan! Answer me!" John Spartan could imagine what his chief looked like right at that moment. He probably had a strangle lock on the mike and his face was bright crimson.

"Do you hear me, Spartan?"

Spartan reached forward and snapped off the

radio. "No," he said. Calmly, he went back to checking the equipment stuffed into his flak vest.

It was Lamb's turn to try and impose some discipline on his fellow policeman. He half turned in his seat and confronted Spartan face to face. "I ain't landing this thing," he said firmly. "You hear *me*?"

"I hear you," murmured Spartan. "Did you hear me asking you to put down?"

"And I'm gonna make sure that you are not gonna go crossing direct district command."

Spartan just shrugged and returned to his pre-operation checklist.

"And I am not going to watch you get your ass shot off," said Lamb grimly.

Spartan looked the pilot in the eye. "Who said that was going to happen?"

"You're facing Simon Phoenix alone, aren't you?" replied Lamb evenly.

The ghost of a smile crossed Spartan's lips. "Hey, Lamb, thanks for the pep talk. Just get me in for a closer look, that's all."

Lamb turned to face forward and cut the chopper's height by a couple of hundred feet. "Close enough?"

Spartan nodded. "That's good."

He returned to the open door and pulled a coiled rope from the canvas bag. Stenciled along the thick line were four letters: LAFD—Los Angeles Fire Department.

Lamb looked confused. "Isn't that thing s'posed to be used for getting people *out* of burning buildings?"

Spartan smiled while he hooked the lifeline to his

chest harness and then clipped a carabineer clasp to the big eyebolt by the door of the chopper.

He nodded. "Yeah, that's what they're used for—generally."

The chopper was hovering over the fortress, and it rocked and bucked as waves of hot air slammed into the undercarriage of the aircraft. The rotors beat flat on scalding air, the engine straining to keep up the lift.

Spartan peered out into the fire storm—and it began to dawn on Lieutenant Lamb just what kind of lunacy his passenger was contemplating.

"Shit, John," Lamb stammered. "You aren't . . . you have got to be kidding me . . ."

This time Spartan grinned. "Send a maniac to catch one. Hang around, will ya?"

And with that, Spartan jumped from the helicopter, free-falling into the inferno.

2

Silently, John Spartan plummeted three hundred feet, a stomach-wrenching free-fall. As the downward force of gravity met the upward pull of the helicopter, Spartan stopped dead in the air just ten feet above the top floor of the building. He snatched a bowie knife from his belt and slashed the cord above his head, dropped noiselessly to the tar roof, rolled, and came up with a gun locked in each fist.

There was a lookout on the roof, standing a few yards to the right, and Spartan was on him in a split second, slamming into the big man. His left hand came up, and he hit the side of the lookout's head with the full force of the six-pound tempered steel revolver. The bad guy never knew what hit him, and he dropped to the floor without a whimper.

Spartan sensed another man, this one to his left,

so he ducked, rolled fast across the tar paper roof, and came up swinging. A fast, steel reinforced, left-right combination put the second lookout's lights out in less than a second.

Spartan wasn't even breathing hard—not yet anyway.

He dropped to one knee and listened for footsteps, his eyes scanning the desolate roofscape for the slightest movement. There was no sound save for the crackling of the fires on the ground and the clatter of the chopper now riding seven hundred and fifty feet above him. If Phoenix knew Spartan had dropped in, he gave no sign of it.

John Spartan holstered his guns. Then he dashed silently for the hatch that opened into the stairwell of the old building, pulling the rusty metal cover from its hinges. He shimmied down the steel ladder, then plunged the last few feet to the floor, stopping to check once again for the enemy.

As far as Spartan could tell, the interior of the fortress was devoid of people, but the vast space was far from empty. Stacked from floor to ceiling stood crates of weapons, M 70 machine gun-grenade launchers looted from a National Guard armory somewhere in the Southlands. There were boxes and boxes of ammunition, enough bullets and grenades to supply an entire infantry brigade for a month's worth of heavy fighting.

In addition to weaponry, Spartan saw that Phoenix had collected tons of luxury goods looted from the rich enclaves of Beverly Hills and Westwood in the first few days of Riot III. Spartan gazed at the boxes of pillaged electronics equipment, jewelry, and liquor and decided there and then that Phoenix would not live to enjoy his ill-gotten booty.

There was a sound of a footfall deep in the warehouse, and Spartan darted toward it, crouching low and tensing like a piece of sprung steel. He paused at the intersection of two avenues of packing crates and peered around the corner.

The guard was right in front of him, and Spartan looked at the man's broad back and bull neck, planning his attack. John Spartan leaped, launching himself from the concrete floor, the full weight of his body slamming into the guard. The man flew forward and smacked his head on the sharp corner of one of the heavy wooden packing crates. Then Spartan pounded the man's bloody forehead against the cold, unforgiving concrete.

The guard went out like a snuffed candle—and he lay so still, so inert that it was obvious that he was not going to be getting up again for a long, long time.

But Spartan had company . . .

Another large lookout dove at Spartan from behind, but he hardly made contact before Spartan used the man's considerable momentum to fling him—splat!—into the wall. Spartan fell on him and landed a flurry of rib-shattering blows. The guard's eyes turned up in his head, and he passed out from the sudden onslaught of shock and pain.

Spartan ran for the stairwell, but the instant he burst through the door, he had to throw himself flat as a series of machine-gun bullets ripped the concrete wall just above his head, showering him with cinder-block chips. The two revolvers roared, the

explosions deafening in the enclosed space. All four
bullets found their target, slamming into the chest
of the guard. The machine-gun fire stopped
abruptly.

"So much for my warm welcome," growled Spartan. He was on his way to the center of the building,
the nerve center of the criminal complex.

He knew that the gunfire would rouse the whole
building, but there was nothing he could do about
it. He had made as many silent kills as he could,
now it was time for some violent gunplay rock and
roll.

It was time to get going, to get on with the
business of rescuing the hostages—and eradicating
Simon Phoenix. A few more guards stood between
Spartan and his quarry, but the judicious use of fists
and fire power took care of them.

Spartan's footsteps echoed in the dim interior,
and he threw himself into the next chamber. He
could tell by the smell in the room that he was close
to Phoenix—not that the outlaw smelled any worse
or better than anyone else, but because the entire
room reeked of spilled gasoline, hundreds of gallons
of it. Doubtless, it was one of Phoenix's ingenious
defense mechanisms. Let the gas flow and blow to
smithereens anyone who tried to take him alive.

Suddenly, what little light penetrated the murky
room vanished as someone—and Spartan could
guess who—hit all the circuit breakers, eliminating
electricity to the complex.

Spartan whispered into his lapel microphone.
"Lamb? You read me?"

"Yeah, Spartan, I read you." Lieutenant Lamb
sounded annoyed. "What the hell is going on?"

"I need you to shed some light on the situation," said Spartan.

"Roger that."

Spartan heard the helicopter engines distinctly as the chopper lost a couple of hundred feet and passed across the building. The thirty-two-million-candle-power lights mounted on the chopper skids kicked in. A split second later a great avalanche of cool white light poured through the tall windows, illuminating the interior of the building.

The room became a wild mixture of burnished white light and where it could not penetrate, dark, dark shadows. The gas fumes seemed to be alive, rippling and refracting, the light bouncing off multi-colored pools of gasoline.

A heart-stopping sound came from the far side of the room. Simon Phoenix, half hidden in the shadows, lit a blowtorch and the sound of the roaring flame seemed to fill the gas-filled chamber. Nonchalantly, the criminal put a cigarette in his mouth and lit it.

The blue flame of the blowtorch illuminated Phoenix's features. It wasn't the kind of face you saw every day. The master criminal was a tall, powerfully built black man, with a deep brown eye—the other one was blue. His hair wasn't black, but had been dyed a garish platinum blond.

"Don't move, Phoenix," Spartan ordered. Both of his heavy weapons were trained on the bad guy.

Phoenix's lips twisted into a smile. "Move? I won't move. I wouldn't want to get gasoline on my shoes."

The flammable liquid was pooling all over the floor now, and the air was becoming thick with choking fumes. In spite of himself, Spartan's eyes flicked down to Phoenix's shoes and then back to his face.

"You're under—"

"Arrest?" Phoenix finished for him.

"That's right."

"Ooooh," said Simon Phoenix laughing in Spartan's face. "I'm scared. And you are trespassing."

Spartan did not have time for cop-criminal banter. "Where are the passengers?"

Phoenix's phony good humor vanished. "Fuck you, Spartan!" His voice echoed to the rafters of the room. "The passengers? The passengers are gone, man. I *told* the city no one comes down here anymore."

"You didn't tell me," said Spartan.

"Why the fuck should I?" demanded Phoenix. "All the other cops figured it out, Goddamn *mailman* could figure it out. Damn bus drivers wouldn't listen."

Spartan shrugged. "Doesn't matter. You're under arrest."

Phoenix looked at the cop as if he had lost his mind. "Arrest me? You've got no jurisdiction here. You're in my kingdom now, Spartan. Fifty blocks in every direction. And it's all mine. Every square inch. Got it?"

Spartan shook his head. "Wrong, Phoenix. Your rent is overdue and I'm your eviction notice."

Phoenix laughed lightly. "Oh, *I* get it. You're gonna be my judge!" He drew on the cigarette and exhaled a long, blue stream of hot smoke.

"That's right."

"Seems like you're slumming to me, Spartan."

"I've never been particular about the people I bring in, Phoenix. You can't be too choosy in my line of work. Scumbags sorta go with the territory."

Phoenix shifted the blowtorch from one hand to the other, tossing it playfully in his large fist. "I'm not going to give up my kingdom to go back to living in a cage. You really want to bring me in, Spartan?"

Spartan never took his eyes off Phoenix's face. "There's an option I would prefer," he said. "But the law says I have to arrest you before I kill you. Understand?"

Phoenix nodded. "I understand. I understand that the only way you're gonna take me is to reach down my throat and tear out my heart."

Spartan nodded, as if Phoenix were giving him an alternative he hadn't considered. "I ain't a doctor, but I'll give it a try. Tell me where the hostages are—and then you should prepare for surgery."

"To hell with the hostages," Phoenix snarled. "This is about you and me, Spartan."

John Spartan's guns had not wavered an inch. He could have blown him away at any moment, but the law said he had to arrest him, and Spartan had to admit that he would derive a curious pleasure from putting Phoenix in that cage he feared so much.

Suddenly, Phoenix snuffed out the blowtorch, the blue flame slowly hissing dead.

"Is it cold in here," Phoenix asked, with a smile, "or is it just me?" Without warning, he took the cigarette from his mouth and flicked it casually at Spartan.

A sheet of blue flame erupted and Phoenix screamed with crazy laughter. Spartan threw himself through the blaze, grappling with Phoenix, try-

ing to drag him through one of the windows—
Spartan figuring that it was better to take a chance
in a fall than to stay inside and fry.

But Phoenix was either stronger, crazier, or whatever drug he had taken made him invincible. He
caught Spartan and smashed him into the wall, then
catching him in the middle of the chest with his
knee.

The heat in the building was overpowering, and
the loose ammunition on the upper floors was beginning to explode, detonating in strings like lethal
fireworks. The two men squared off and traded
blows, toe to toe, like boxers in the ring, bone-
crunching, brain-rocking punches.

Neither man could bring down the other until
Phoenix broke out, aiming—and landing—a vicious
kick to Spartan's head, as if trying to snap his head
off his spine.

"That feel good?" screamed Phoenix. "Let me
take a little bit off the left . . ." He ripped another
brutal kick, sending Spartan reeling.

Spartan swayed on his feet, shaking his head
trying to clear his mind.

"Dizzy, Spartan? How many fingers am I holding
up?" Phoenix held two long-nailed fingers under
Spartan's battered head and then savagely rammed
them into his eyes, sending him crashing to the
ground. Phoenix raised his foot, ready to stomp
Spartan's head into the concrete.

But this time Spartan was ready for him. His legs
swept out and slammed into Phoenix, whipping him
to the ground, and suddenly Spartan was on his feet
slamming and kicking, nailing Phoenix three times
fast in the face and body. The skin on his cheek-

bones split and blood flowed, pooling on the concrete floor.

Spartan stood over his fallen enemy. "Where are they, Phoenix? Where are the hostages?"

Simon Phoenix manage to pull himself up, half rising off the floor. He spat blood and teeth and flashed a gory, crooked smile at the policeman.

"Oh, you want the *hostages*! Why didn't you say so?" He pantomimed patting his pockets, as if looking for his car keys. "Now where did I put them? I swear, I'd lose my head if it wasn't attached . . ."

"I'll keep that in mind," said Spartan, moving in for the kill. Spartan hammered the bruised man with a mighty blow. The sound of his jaw cracking could be heard above the roar of the flames and the intensifying explosions of the loose ammunition rounds. Phoenix's head snapped back, and Spartan grabbed him by the collar and started dragging him from the building. He knew enough about explosives to realize that the whole building was just seconds away from detonating.

It took fifteen seconds for Spartan to get his captive out of the building and undercover. Five seconds later the flames reached the grenades and other explosives on the third floor and ignited. The earth seemed to tremble as the explosion erupted and the heat surge washed forward like a fiery tidal wave. The roar was deafening, and the fire ball that blasted into the sky seemed brighter than the sun.

The secondary explosion was just as devastating, a great eruption of blazing power that blew out the walls of the building. In a matter of seconds Phoenix's fortress was a blazing ruin.

For a city grown inured to explosions, this one was pretty spectacular. It might even make the evening news.

John Spartan had blazed the trail in, so now the Los Angeles Police Department Hum-Vee units were converging on the scene. The air was alive with helicopter traffic, beams of light streaming from the sky.

The dust began to settle, but flaming wreckage and embers still blew from the ruins. Fully armed firemen wearing bulletproof gear were advancing into the wreckage, securing the area and searching for survivors.

Spartan emerged from his cover, dragging his prisoner behind him, handing him off to the crowd of police officers who had rushed to the site. In the middle of the pack of cops was Steve Healy, Spartan's long-suffering superior and friend. He was shaking his head slowly . . . Spartan knew that was always a bad sign.

"Do you understand the meaning of the word 'not', John?" asked Healy. "It's a simple word. Just three letters long." Healy was trying to keep his anger in check, but it appeared to be a losing battle. His face was getting red—another bad sign.

"You were *not* supposed to come down here," he said, his voice rising. "You were *not* supposed to attempt an arrest of Simon Phoenix single-handed, and you were *not* supposed to blow anything up!"

Spartan shrugged. "Not this time, Healy," he said in his own defense. "He dumped gas and rigged the place to blow. Not my fault."

Healy knew Spartan's penchant for blowing

things up too well to be convinced by this lame excuse. "Yeah. Sure. You had nothing to do with it."

"Really," protested Spartan.

"Save it, John," said Healy. "Now I know you've been trying to nail this psycho for two years, but try remembering a little thing called official police procedure."

Spartan winced and slapped his forehead. "Procedure! Damn! I always forget that."

"I know. Now where are the hostages?"

"Not here," said Spartan simply.

Healy frowned. "What the hell do you mean, not here? You come in here, blow the shit out of the place, and you tell me that the hostages aren't here?"

Spartan nodded. "That's right. Phoenix must have stashed them somewhere else."

"You searched the whole place?" Healy demanded. "How do you know they weren't in there. How can you be so sure?"

"We did a thermal check," Spartan explained. "We read only seven bodies—all part of his gang."

"Wrong again."

Healy and Spartan turned. Simon Phoenix was cuffed and trussed and just about to be lead away by a posse of heavily armed police officers.

Spartan grabbed a handful of Phoenix's shirt front. "Then where are they, scumbag?"

Phoenix just grinned.

"Get him out of here," ordered Healy. "Now, Spartan, you and I are going to have a nice long chat—"

Suddenly, one of the fireman rooting around in

the wreckage called out. "Captain! Captain!" The man sounded shocked and sickened. "Over here! There are bodies everywhere. They must be twenty or thirty, they're everywhere!"

Spartan stood stock-still, a sickened look crossing his face. Phoenix dug in his heels and turned to face Healy.

"They were there and he knew it," Phoenix shouted. "I told him and he said he didn't care."

Spartan lost it. He charged Phoenix, his hands out like claws ready to choke the life from his archenemy. A half dozen cops got between them.

Phoenix laughed again. "See! He's crazy. How could you sacrifice innocent people for me? Huh, Spartan? What kind of man are you? I get the feeling we're gonna be spending a lot of quality time together, Spartan."

"I'll kill you," vowed John Spartan.

"Nawww," said Phoenix with a big grin. "We're gonna get to be good friends . . ." The cops hustled him toward the armored Hum-Vee paddy wagon.

Healy looked very grim. He turned to Spartan, real concern on his face. He knew that Phoenix, crazy as he may be, was certainly telling the truth. No one was going to sit still for a cop causing the death of thirty innocent people.

"I'm sorry, John," Healy said quietly. "But if you've got a lawyer, you better call him."

3

By 1996 one thing had improved—by necessity, the criminal justice system had been streamlined. Trials were brief, appeals were perfunctory, and punishment, for the few malefactors the police did manage to apprehend, was swift and appalling.

State and federal penitentiaries had been crammed to the point of overflowing, and after a series of extremely violent prison riots and take-overs, the constitutional right against cruel and un-usual punishment had been abrogated. Thus an institution called the Cryo-Penitentiary was born.

High-risk prisoners, incorrigible and violent crim-inals, were now sentenced to long terms of incarcer-ation not in conventional prisons, but in high-tech establishments where prisoners were not just con-fined but frozen in suspended animation.

Technology had advanced to the point that heart rate and brain activity could be slowed, putting criminals in an inert state of hibernation. The authorities called it "Sub-zero rehabilitation." On the street, it was known as "doing ice" or "ice time."

After a kangaroo court convicted John Spartan, he got seventy years' ice time. He expected as much and hardly flinched when the sentence was read out in court. Spartan accepted that his own life was over—he had worked too long in criminal justice to actually *expect* justice—but he was sickened by what the stigma of his penalty might do to his family.

On the day Spartan was due to begin his term of incarceration, the authorities allowed him a moment or two to say good-bye to his wife and little daughter. He was dressed in stark white prison overalls, and he did his best to hide his shame from the only two people in his life who mattered to him.

Katie, his six-year-old daughter, was doing her best to be strong, but she couldn't fight back the tears that streamed down her face. Spartan bent down and embraced the little girl, kissing her warmly.

"Daddy," she said, "please don't go."

"It won't be long, Katie," he said softly. He opened his hand and showed her his Los Angeles Police Department badge. Then he pinned it to her lapel. "Take care of this for me, till I come back."

Katie nodded solemnly. "Okay."

"I'm going to be back," he said reassuringly. "I'll still be your dad. I promise." He kissed her on the cheek. "Take care of your mom. Will you do that for me?"

The little girl nodded again. "Uh-huh. I love you, Daddy."

Seeing his daughter trying to be brave and strong was almost too much for Spartan, and it was all he could do to choke back the sob that rose in his throat. His wife, Madeline, hugged him close.

"Your mother told you to never marry a cop," said John Spartan over her shoulder.

"I never listen to my mother," said Madeline Spartan, doing her best to smile through her tears.

"I love you," said John Spartan.

They kissed again and held each other in silence. Everything that could be said had been said.

Behind them came the sharp rasp of the metal doors of the cell being opened. Two prison guards dressed in odd heavily insulated uniforms came into the room.

"It's time, Spartan," said one of the men.

John Spartan kissed his wife and daughter one last time and then turned and squared his shoulders.

"Let's go."

The guards, standing on either side of him, escorted him through the metal doors and into the prison proper. The Cryo-Penitentiary was a nightmare of sharp angles and barren white planes, like a pile of geodesic domes stacked one on top of another. It was an architecturally perverse collection of layers and levels with the ambience and all the charm of an industrial-size high-tech meat locker.

The air was cold, and the breath of the few men gathered in the main chamber sent clouds of condensation drifting toward the exposed steel beams of the rafters.

Spartan had never been inside the Cryo-Penitentiary before, but he was well aware of its fearsome reputation. On the lower levels of the space, embedded in the clear Lucite floor, were hundreds of circular units, every one containing the body of a prisoner, frozen within like an insect preserved in amber.

The bodies had contracted into tortured, twisted crouches, grown men coiled into gruesome parodies of the fetal position. They lay with their eyes open, their pale faces hauntingly twisted into gargoylelike expressions of tortured terror.

The operators of the Cryo-Penitentiary knew that it was pointless to try and fight the medication that reduced men to this piteous state, that struggling against it only intensified and made more painful the procedure. And yet, to a man the cryo-cons resisted, struggling against the state-sponsored waking death as strongly as they would the old-fashioned, more primal kind of extinction. It was in their nature to resist authority, even from beyond the grave.

A small group of men waited for Spartan, and they were standing in a half circle around the edge of one of the exposed chambers, which gaped in the floor of the prison like an open grave. A bank of monitors glowed nearby, and two supervisors stood over the instruments, checking and rechecking every stage of the operation.

Called in to observe the proceedings were a couple of police officials, a medical crew, some technical operators, and a young man named Smithers, a rising star in the Bureau of Prisons—he had already achieved the distinction of being named the warden of the first Cryo-Penitentiary. A remarkable achievement, considering his age.

A guard shoved Spartan into the pit and stepped back to let the technicians take over. Spartan knew the drill. Once in the cavity he started unbuttoning his white jumpsuit and stepped free of it, naked in the frigid air.

A doctor stepped forward with a nightmarishly large syringe in his hands, the cylinder filled with a luminescent deep blue liquid. Spartan did not flinch as the needle sliced into his skin and buried itself deep in muscle tissue, nor did he react as the physician pumped the fluid into him.

Technicians gathered around him, like mechanics working on a car, slapping sensor pads on his rapidly cooling body and, to accelerate the chilling process, sprayed him down with icy Freon mist. Immediately, the gauges responded, reflecting the sudden drop in John Spartan's body temperature.

Warden Smithers stepped forward, a small piece of paper in his hand. He cleared his throat portentously, as if he was about to speak words of great import. "John Spartan," he said. "You've done great deeds for the city of Los Angeles. So it is with some regret that I am required to hereby—"

"Skip it," growled Spartan. He was shivering uncontrollably now, and his arms and legs were stiffening, the muscles bulging under his skin as if his body was actually turning to ice.

Smithers stopped, cleared his throat again and gave it another try.

"John Spartan," he said, his voice ringing in the icy chamber. "You have been sentenced to seventy years sub-zero rehabilitation in the California Cryo-

Penitentiary. Your crime is the involuntary man-slaughter of thirty—''

''Skip it,'' Spartan ordered.

The last thing he needed to hear before voyaging into eternity was a recitation of his crime—even if it had been a horrible mistake. He would maintain his innocence even if he was forced to take it with him to his frozen grave.

He was beginning to shake with the cold now, great racking shudders, chemical-induced tremors that shook his whole body. The blood in his face had drained away, leaving his skin a severe parchment white, the only color in his face the burning intensity of his dark eyes and the ice blue of his lips.

Spartan—no surprise—was not performing like the other men who had shared his horrible fate. They had screamed and twisted on their cold, subterranean gallows, desperately trying to break free. Spartan fought the process, too, but not with his body—it was too late for that, a futile waste of energy. Spartan resisted with his mind.

But he was going under, and no one now had the power to change his destiny. Smithers shook his head ruefully as if he genuinely regretted the duty he was forced to perform.

''I'm sorry, John,'' he said. ''An order is an order, you know. If you had realized that a long time ago, you wouldn't be standing here now.''

John Spartan summoned up all the strength he could muster, forcing his lips and tongue to function.

''Thanks for the advice,'' he managed to croak. ''I'll bear it in mind.''

Smithers flashed him a cruel smile. "Don't go catching cold, Demolition Man."

"Fuh . . . fuh . . . funny." The single word required superhuman effort.

One of the technicians hit a button on the console, and John Spartan sank into the cryonic chamber.

"See you next century," said Smithers with a grin. "Sleep tight."

The casing door closed over John Spartan, and the monitors and gauges began spitting out information. Spartan's cryo-file was opened with that day's date, the date of completion of sentence, and the date of theoretical parole.

There was no policy on early release because the question had not yet arisen. Not one of the frozen inmates had served close to even a small portion of his sentence, and the authorities had as yet to decide what constituted time reduction for good behavior. Of course it was difficult to assess the conduct of a group of formerly violent, homicidal men now frozen as stiff as a bunch of fish sticks.

The rest of the cryogenic process inside Spartan's pod was computer controlled. A superchilled clear gel flooded into the compartment, molding to Spartan's body, packing and preserving his rigid figure.

Spartan was still barely conscious, aware that this process had entered a new phase. A mechanical arm delivered a small white chip into the center of the gel. The interaction of the fragment and the gel brought the process to a close. In an instant the sludge froze solid, as rock hard as a diamond, the opposite of watching ice shatter.

The temperature readout dropped until it read

one half of one degree above zero degrees Kelvin. In the last second before the chamber froze over, John Spartan's face contorted, but not into a rictus of fear or dread, but into a defiant sneer.

4

Violent crime remained a growth industry for the remainder of the twentieth century and well into the twenty-first. With the extraordinary proliferation of vicious malfeasance came the ever-increasing development of cryo-penology—another booming growth industry. Consequently, California Cryo-Penitentiary X23-1, the facility in which John Spartan had been incarcerated back in 1996, had by the year 2032 grown to three times its original size.

One thing had not changed. Smithers was still warden of the complex. His bright career in the prison system had stalled some time in the second decade of the new century, and the great future that had been predicted for him all those years ago had never come to pass.

He was a gray-haired old man now, the absolute

ruler of his cold, silent kingdom, but he was embittered by his fate and resentful of the success of others promoted over his head to jobs more important than his own, assignments he considered to be his rightfully, had it not been for the ineptitude and stupidity of his superiors.

But Smithers was, by nature, breeding, and training, a career technocrat, and he performed his duties to the letter or the rule book, even to the point of pointlessness.

When his compuclipboard buzzed early one Monday morning, he knew who was calling and why. And like a loyal servant of the state he had all his information marshaled and ready.

The ultraflat-screen video monitor on his compuclipboard burst into life, revealing the head and shoulders of Lieutenant Lenina Huxley, an officer of the SAPD—the mega law-enforcement agency known as the San Angeles Police Department.

"Mellow greetings, Warden William Smithers," she said.

This again, thought Smithers. For thirty-six years he had been going through this same routine, always on Mondays.

"Yeah," said Smithers. "Be well, Lieutenant Lenina Huxley."

Of course Smithers hadn't been reporting to Lieutenant Huxley for thirty-six years. The attractive young woman was still in her early twenties and didn't mind looking at her face on the monitor—it was her attitude he couldn't stand.

Huxley had jet black hair, cut short in a pageboy that brushed her slim shoulders. Her skin was flawless and smooth, and her dark, almond-shaped eyes were wide set and stared out of the monitor in amusement.

There was a mischievousness about her lips, something that suggested that in private, she was disdainful of authority. But that was not the sort of thing that you let show in the brave new world.

Lieutenant Lenina Huxley was talking to Warden Smithers from her bubblelike police cruiser, which was gliding down an absolutely spic-and-span city street. Every building she passed was in good repair, and every inch of the sidewalk was swept clean. Other emissionless cars hummed by, the drivers observing to the letter every traffic rule, and no one even dared to think of exceeding the speed limit.

"As it is a beautiful Monday morning," said Huxley, "and as my duty log irrationally requires it. . . ." Lenina looked into the mirror of her car and fussed with her hair, using both hands. Cars did not require anything as primitive as a steering wheel. You could use one if you chose to, if a feeling of control was required, but very few people bothered.

". . . I am hereby querying you on the prison population update." Satisfied with her appearance, she looked away from the mirror. "Does the tedium continue, Warden Smithers?"

Smithers smiled sardonically at the image on his board as he walked through his silent kingdom.

"Your earnest questionage is as amusing as it is irrelevant, Lieutenant," he said, talking directly to the compuclipboard in his hands.

"Is it?" asked Lenina Huxley.

"You know it is," snapped Smithers. "The pri-

soners are ice cubes. They do not move. They have
no thoughts; they have no feelings. Their criminal
instincts are being reprogrammed as they sleep. The
process of reform is slow and monotonous. Therefore, Lieutenant, the tedium is almost permanent.''

Lenina Huxley frowned. ''I find this lack of stim-
ulus truly disappointing. As officers of our law-
enforcement agency, I would imagine our lives
should be a bit more exciting. Don't you think,
Warden?''

Smithers peered at the young woman, real suspi-
cion in his eyes.

''I try not to, Lieutenant,'' he said. In fact, if he
had his way, thinking would be outlawed—after all,
virtually everything else had been.

''Is that so, Warden Smithers?''

''Yes it is,'' said the older man. ''Of course you
are young and you may think all you want. Things
don't *happen* anymore. We've taken care of all
that.'' He looked around the cavernous interior of
the prison, at the thousands of units containing
cryogenically suspended prisoners. ''Everything
runs smoothly. That's the way things are supposed
to be. No surprises. No crime.''

And it is so boring, thought Huxley.

''I'll have to fiber-op you back after the morning
nonparole hearings, Lieutenant,'' he said, doing his
best to sound busy. ''Have a peachy day, and be
well.'' His image vanished from the screen in a poof
of static.

''Same to you,'' grumbled Lenina Huxley.

Warden Smithers walked to the entrance of the
secure area and placed the back of his hand onto a
screen set in the wall. Almost instantly, a female

voice spoke to him, a voice so perfectly modulated
to be smooth and cheery yet devoid of emotion that
it could only be produced by a computer.

"Coding accepted," the machine said. "Retina
confirm, please."

Smithers leaned forward, placing his left eye
against a peephole embedded in the wall next to the
hand scanner. A red laser beam passed across the
Warden's eye, reading the configuration of colors
and imperfections in his retina, an individual char-
acteristic more particular to a single human being
than a fingerprint. A retina scan could not be forged,
fudged, or duplicated. It was thought to be fool-
proof.

The laser matched the eye to a series of codes
entered in the security computer. It checked out
and the door opened silently, a section of wall
sliding away.

"Thank you and be well, Warden William Smithers," said the computer voice.

Two guards flanked the barely conscious cryo-
prisoner who was strapped into a lustrous and uncomfortable wheelchair. The seat was made of
gleaming titanium, but its design looked peculiarly
archaic, a throwback to the long-ago nineteenth
century, a time when prisoners were restrained in
such devices.

Smithers dropped behind his desk and flicked on
his compuclipboard. He got right down to the business of the parole hearing. Shortly after the cryo-
detention of John Spartan, the California Correc-
tional Commission did get around to working out
parole guidelines for prisoners who had been sub-
jected to the cryo-discipline. As the United States

Constitution was still suspended, the CCC had come up with a simple piece of public policy: There was no parole—never—for anyone.

However, Warden Smithers had to go through the motions of explaining this to hurriedly thawed prisoners. It was largely a waste of time, but Warden Smithers had plenty of time on his hands.

As the groggy prisoner tried to focus on what was going on around him, Smithers read from his clipboard. "Twenty-nine years ago the parole system as you knew it was rendered obsolete."

"Huh?" said the prisoner.

"Federal Statute 537-29 requires that we go through the formality of a hearing for all prisoners incarcerated before the repeal of the parole laws."

"Who?"

"Cocteau Behavioral Engineering, B.E., will continue rehabilitation by altering your behavior through synaptic suggestion during cryogenic-induced sleep. Nightie night," said Smithers. "Your hearing is now over."

"Wha?" The prisoner was making feeble attempts to get out of his chair. The guards could have restrained him with a single finger.

"You are to be returned to your cryo-cell immediately." Smithers looked down at his compuclipboard. "Do you understand what I've just said, Mr. . . . Horace Bateman?"

His eyes half open, Horace Bateman attempted to find the right words to say. He didn't want to go back to sleep. He would do anything to avoid that. Go to regular pen—go straight if he could convince the law that his lawless, recidivist days were done for good.

Smithers didn't want to hear about it. He drummed his fingers on his desk, waiting for Bateman's response. But the hapless man was still groping for the right words to beg and plead for mercy.

"Guards," said Smithers impatiently, "nod his head for him, please."

One of the guards grabbed a handful of the prisoner's cold, sweaty hair and nodded the man's head.

"Thank you, Mr. Bateman. See you in six years." He did not attempt to stifle his yawn or conceal his boredom. "Next, please."

Two medical technicians—med techs in prison argot—pulled a prisoner from his pod and loaded his still unconscious form onto one of the wheelchairs. There was something familiar about him, something from the long dead past. The prisoner had a well-muscled body, black skin, and blond hair. . . .

Lieutenant Lenina Huxley decided she would drive. She pressed a button on the dashboard of her police cruiser, and a steering wheel emerged from its compartment and locked into place. She coded her badge into the computer in the console.

"Huxley," she said. "Lenina. Coding on for activation instructions."

The same serenely annoying voice that cleared Warden Smithers through his security check responded to her. "No police presence is requested in the city at this time. Report to your station. Good morning, Officer Huxley."

Lenina moaned softly. *Boring.* "Oh wow," she said aloud. "How exciting."

But the computer voice had not gone away. "I

detect a promoted level of stress in your tone. Would you like me to prescribe a foodaceutical to assist in mood elevation?"

"No!" snapped Lenina Huxley. "What are you? My mother?" Lenina immediately tried to calm her voice. You could get in real trouble if you sassed a computer. The little sneaks . . .

"I mean, no. But thank you for caring." She rolled her eyes and waited to see if she would get a scolding. But the rebuke was not forthcoming.

"All right," she said. "Reporting in."

It was going to be another exciting day in paradise. Or so she thought.

5

Lenina Huxley's route to work took her right by a lengthy, block-long expanse of whitewashed wall that encircled a hospital. In the bad old days an expanse of pure white like this would have attracted the immediate attention of slogan writers and graffiti artists, culture or eyesore, depending on one's politics and sense of aesthetics.

In the new world the wall merely remained pristine, undefiled white. Until that morning . . .

Despite draconian litter laws, none of the San Angelenos noticed that just that morning, standing in front of the enticing white wall was a small round, tin object about the size and shape of a coffee can. Odder still, no one noticed that the can was ticking . . .

Abruptly, the ticking stopped to be followed by a

small, sharp explosion that sprayed a series of multicolored inks on to the wall, frescoing a crudely painted message. It read: LIFE FROM HELL—BE.

Pedestrians stopped and gaped, their mouths open, aghast that anyone should have sought to upset public order in such a disgraceful, disrespectful and deceitful manner. The passersby looked around, half expecting to see dark clouds heralding the end of the world rising over the Hollywood Hills.

But the apocalypse was forestalled by two shock poles that emerged from the wall, dropped into place, and generated a cleansing burst of lightning that burned the message off the wall. The shock poles retreated into their slots, and no one would have been the wiser.

Except the mayhem didn't end there . . .

In the middle of the street a manhole popped open, and a crude periscope emerged just as a food truck pulled into the lot nearby. Workmen got busy unloading the food modules, the whole operation observed by the young man under the street.

"All right," he whispered, "that's it. In twelve hours there will be another delivery." Edgar Friendly pulled off his glasses and wiped them on his ancient, greasy mechanic's overalls, then returned his eye to the periscope.

"Good, glorious food. In twelve hours they'll be back . . ." He shook his head of wild, uncombed hair in wonderment. "These assholes are nothing if not predictable. God, how I love hating this place."

There were two other young men with him, crouching in the sewer pipe. They looked just as disreputable as their leader. There were some people, the young and disenfranchised, normally, who couldn't or wouldn't fit into the sterile world above them. Collectively, they were known as the Scraps, leftover from the perfect, regulated society they refused to join.

They were dirty and wild, but they were alive in ways that the upper people would never understand. But there was a downside. They were hunted, hated, and hungry—food supply was strictly controlled and doled out only to those who conformed.

"Tomorrow, we strike!" said Edgar.

His fellow Scraps exchanged worried looks. "We're not ready, Friendly."

"Hey, Mason, it doesn't really matter if we're ready or not anymore. We've got nothing to lose . . ." He shrugged. "Except maybe our lives."

Edgar Friendly withdrew the periscope and dropped down into the sewer. "Well, let's go. Things to do," said Friendly. "People to see . . ."

No one from the bad old days would have recognized the police station where Lieutenant Lenina Huxley was based. It was softly lit, impeccably neat and, most shocking of all, almost completely silent. Needless to say, there were no criminals—anywhere. They were not sitting at desks giving statements, under interrogation, or being hustled into cells.

Police officers of every shape, size, and ethnic origin worked without rush or worry, observing the activity of the city on a vast array of monitors.

The loudest voice in the room—and he barely spoke above a murmur—belonged to Merwin, the impossibly perky dispatcher who spoke into his headset as Lenina Huxley passed.

"Greetings and salutations," he whispered into his microphone. "Welcome to the emergency line of the San Angeles Police Department. If you would prefer an automated response, please press one." Callers almost invariably preferred to talk to a machine.

Lenina Huxley went to her station just as one of her tough-looking colleagues sidled up to her— Lieutenant James MacMillan, widely thought to be the meanest cop in the district. They exchanged nontouching handshakes, each of them making a concentric circle with their open palms.

"Let me guess," said Huxley in disgust. "All is serene, right?"

Her colleague looked shocked. "G and S, Lenina Huxley," MacMillan said. "It's been a brutal morning. There was a defacement of public buildings, not an hour ago. Walls were smudged!"

Lieutenant Huxley's mouth dropped open. She was genuinely astounded. "Really! Brutal. I was just in sector, and I didn't hear any cars notified. I would have thought there would be a bulletin to all of us."

But before her pal could respond, he was cut off by Lenina Huxley's by-the-book superior, Chief George Earle.

"Because there was no need to create widespread panic," he said gruffly.

"Good thinking, Chief," said MacMillan, taking this moment to slip away.

Chief Earle was pleased with that development. He wanted a chance to talk to Lenina.

"Lieutenant Huxley, I monitored your disheartening and distressing comments to Warden Smithers this morning."

Inwardly, Lenina rebuked herself. *Of course* Earle would have been listening in. Why hadn't she thought of that!

"Sorry, sir."

Earle folded his arms across his broad chest. "Do you actually long for chaos and disharmony? Your fascination with the vulgar twentieth century seems to be affecting your better judgment. And, of course, you realize that you're setting a bad example for other officers and personnel."

Lenina Huxley nodded and examined her perfectly shined boots. "Thank you for the attitude readjustment, Chief Earle. The info is assimilated."

Chief Earle turned on his heel. "Good. Keep it up."

Lenina ducked into her office, making a face behind her superior's back. She cursed softly, almost silently, under her breath.

"Sanctimonious asshole," she whispered.

Although almost inaudible, her voice was picked up the morality box on the wall of her office. The box squawked into life.

"Lenina Huxley," droned the box—this was not the soothing computer voice, but a stern instructor like a marine drill sergeant. "You are fined one and a half credits for a sotto voce violation of the verbal morality statute."

The box clicked off as a thin sheet of paper slid out of the machine containing printed confirmation of her violation. The ticket recorded her name, rank, and address, the number of violations she had accumulated to date, and the amount of the deduction from her bank account.

She fought down the anger and screwed up her face, using all her will power not to curse again, this time louder.

"Golly!" she snarled.

In contrast to the rest of the police station, Lenina Huxley's office was quite a surprise. First of all, it was a mess, a riot of papers and food wrappers, quite out of line with the goal of perfect order instilled in all members of the San Angeles Police Department.

But even more amazing than something as subversive as litter, was Lenina's collection of the rare and odd, an accumulation of antiques, curios, and rarities from the past.

The office was jammed with odds and ends, the pop cultural icons of a long dead era, and taken together all of the junk added up to a shrine to the late twentieth century.

There was a giant Wurlitzer juke box packed with hits of the 1950s. The walls were decorated with a dozen faded black-and-white photographs of movie stars whose names and movies were long forgotten. There were fifteen or twenty pairs of athletic shoes, running the gamut from the plastic and canvas high tops through to the more high-tech offerings of the nineties.

There were neon signs and eight track tapes, lava lamps and leisure suits. In a corner was a jumble of old TV sets, VCRs, and hopelessly antiquated personal computers and telephones. Lenina had scoured the junk shops and scrap heaps to find old magazines, newspapers, and comic books. There was even a stack of paperback books, everything from Stephen King's *Gerald's Game* to a tattered Penguin Classics edition of Aldous Huxley's *Brave New World*.

Nothing had escaped her eagle eye for the odds and ends of the past.

Lenina could spend hours puzzling over the faded newsprint, reliving a more exciting time. There was a long procession of plastic characters, animals mostly, that Lenina suspected had something to do with movies: a white duck in a sailor's suit, a jet black mouse with outlandish round ears, a series of dwarves . . .

In the middle of all this clutter sat Lenina's partner, a congenitally sweet-natured man named Alfredo Garcia. He sat at his desk shaking his head, glancing unhappily at the morality box.

"Whew . . ." he said. "That was tense."

Lenina shot him a deadpan glare. "You think that was tense? Tell me something, Garcia, don't you get bored codetracing perps who break curfew and tell dirty jokes?"

"Actually," said Garcia loudly, "now that you ask, I find my job deeply fulfilling." Then he lowered his voice. "I just cannot swallow the reality of this office, Lenina Huxley."

"You can't?"

"No. You're still addicted to the twentieth-century high from its harshness, you're buzzed by its brutality. Holy smokes, is there anything in here which doesn't violate contraband ordinance twenty-two?"

Huxley smiled sweetly. "Just you, Alfredo Garcia. Don't you ever want *something* to happen."

Garcia shook his head. "Goodness. No."

Lenina Huxley sighed heavily. "I knew you were going to say that . . ." She slung herself into her chair and planted her elbows on her desk.

"What I wouldn't give for some action," she said wistfully.

6

Warden William Smithers was slowly working through his roster of prisoners, happily denying parole to a dozen hastily thawed out prisoners. All morning, however, he had been looking forward to the next felon, the most illustrious inmate of California Cryo-Penitentiary X23-1, Simon Phoenix.

The technicians who warmed up Phoenix were surprised that he seemed a little more conscious than usual. He wasn't completely awake, but he was far from the usual semicomatose state of most of the newly awakened prisoners.

They strapped him into the transport chair and wheeled him before the warden. Phoenix was doing his best to shake off his postcryogenic confusion, and he was aware enough that when finally confronted with the warden, he was able to lock eyes with Smithers. The criminal was still menacing after all the frozen years.

William Smithers found himself slightly disconcerted. In all his years as warden he had never encountered a prisoner who seemed to have shaken off the effects of his cryo-sleep so quickly.

The warden's eyes darted to the steel manacles that bound Simon Phoenix firmly to his gurney. They were solidly in place, trussing his body securely, shackling his wrists and ankles, plus another steel band across his midsection and another bond around his neck. Smithers was reassured. No one, not even Phoenix, could worm out of these manacles.

Smithers smiled down at the prisoners. "Mr. Simon Phoenix," he said, "one of our first and most illustrious members. We won't delay you too long."

"Good," said Phoenix.

Smithers was unsettled. Phoenix was glaring at him, his eyes alive with hatred. It was far more reaction than the warden was used to, and Smithers felt a faint, irrational stab of fear. He cleared his throat and started to read from his compuclipboard. The spiel was always the same, and he was sure he could have done it in his sleep, but this morning he needed some place to put his eyes.

"Twenty-nine years ago, the parole system . . ."

"Twenty-nine years ago," repeated Phoenix, "the parole system . . ."

Smithers tried not to be intimidated and he spoke in a firmer tone of voice. ". . . was rendered obsolete . . ."

Phoenix too, made his voice firmer. ". . . was rendered obsolete . . ."

Smithers stood up and smacked Phoenix on the head with his compuclipboard. "Stop it!" he ordered. "Do you have anything fresh to say in your behalf, Mr. Phoenix?"

Phoenix's eyes glittered, but he did not speak.

Smithers's smile was cruel. "I thought not." He turned his back on the prisoner. "The great Simon Phoenix! Not so all powerful now! And nothing to say on your own behalf either." The Warden shook his head. "I'm *verrry* disappointed."

"Actually," said Phoenix, "yeah, I do have something to say . . ." A look of complete puzzlement crossed his face. There was something he had to say, but he had no idea why he wanted to say it. "Teddy bear."

The instant he spoke a loud buzz filled the room, and all six manacles flew open. The guards just gaped, but Simon Phoenix knew a good thing when he saw it. He vaulted out of the wheelchair and slammed a panther kick into the nearest guard, doubling him over.

As the man went down, Phoenix grabbed an air-injected syringe from the guard's holster and slammed the shiny steel needle into the second guard's forehead, skewering the man's brain on the six-inch shaft of metal.

The destruction of the two guards took less than three and a half seconds. Smithers hadn't moved an inch, and somewhere in his brain he knew that there were security procedures that dealt with the unlikely event of a prisoner escape, but he couldn't for the life of him remember what they were. He stood rooted to the spot, gaping dumbstruck at .

"How did you know the password to the cuffs?" stammered Warden Smithers.

Phoenix cackled with pleasure. He didn't *know* how he happened to know the password that opened the manacles—but he didn't give a damn. The point is, he knew and that was good enough for Simon Phoenix.

"I have no idea, Warden . . ." he advanced a few steps on Smithers. The man shrank back in terror. "But I do know that Simon says, too much talking from you."

Suddenly, life returned to the warden's limbs. He made a break for the door, but Phoenix was too fast for him. He struck and struck hard, smashing his left hand into Smithers's larynx, crushing the old man's throat and sending him toppling to the ground. The prisoner fell on his former captor, grinning at him as he snatched a sharp pointed pen from the pocket of Smithers's white lab coat.

"I'll have to take your pen, Warden," he said. "I need a piece of ID." With an evil smile he raised the pen like a dagger and then plunged it straight at Smithers's right eye.

As far as the laser security device knew, Warden William Smithers was presenting himself for retina clearance. The beam passed over the warden's eye and the door clicked open.

"Access granted, Warden William Smithers," said the unflappable computer voice.

Simon Phoenix stepped through the doorway. William Smithers's disembodied bloody eye was clutched in his hand. The laser, of course, had no reason to suspect that Smithers's eye wasn't attached to his body, so the brain granted Phoenix access to the exit passage of the prison.

As he walked away from the security point, he tossed the eye away. It landed with a splat on the steel floor.

"Thank you, Warden William Smithers," said the computer voice. "And be well."

Phoenix glanced at the speaker. The future, what little he had seen of it, was very strange indeed. "Yeah? You be well, too."

Unchallenged, Phoenix strolled out of the austere prison building, crossing a lawn as green and as well tended as a posh country club golf course. Phoenix turned and looked back at the jail and had to admit to himself that it was absolutely the nicest, cleanest, neatest penitentiary he had ever been in. It was also remarkably easy to get out of—all you needed was one lucky break and you were free.

"Now," said Phoenix aloud. "I need to get me some sharp transport."

The prison parking lot was empty save for a single man in a white coat just getting into his very sharp-looking sports car. Phoenix dashed over to him.

"Excuse me, mac," said Phoenix. "Are you going my way, by any chance?"

The prison worker smiled, but shook his head. "I might be, friend, but there's a problem. My vehicle only seats one person. I'm sorry."

Phoenix smiled just as affably. "That's not a problem."

"No?" asked the man, puzzled.

"Well, not for *me*." Phoenix's hands sprung out

and seized the man by the neck. In a matter of seconds he had choked the life from him, his hands seemingly charged with superhuman strength. The delicate bones in the throat cracked and splintered under his powerful grasp, and the man's eyes bugged from his skull, his tongue lolling obscenely from his mouth.

Phoenix let his victim drop and looked at his hands. "I don't remember being this strong," he said. "Just goes to show what happens after a good night's sleep."

He got into the car and instinctively knew how to operate the vehicle. He drove away, a big smile on his face. He was having a *very* good day.

In the dispatch room of Lenina Huxley's police station a sensor on the giant electronic map of the entire, vast city of San Angeles snapped on suddenly and glowed bright.

The serene computer voice came from a speaker mounted above the map. "One eight seven, one eight seven, one eight seven, one eight seven . . ."

The cops in the room didn't notice the voice droning in the background at first; they were too busy attending to the routine chores of the station house to pay attention to anything out of the ordinary.

It was Merwin, the dispatcher, who finally observed the red dot on the map and the series of digits endlessly repeated.

"What's a one eight seven?" he asked Lieutenant MacMillan, who happened to be standing nearby.

"Search me," said the tough-looking cop.

Merwin punched the code into his computer keyboard. He stared at the monitor for a split second, then slumped in his chair, fainting dead away.

"Merwin!" shouted MacMillan, "what's the matter?" Then *he* caught sight of the notation on the screen. The color drained from his face.

"Oh my, oh my, oh my," said MacMillan, holding his face in his hands and rocking back and forth like an infant in need of a big, warm hug. "I don't believe it!"

Lenina Huxley and Alfredo Garcia were just returning from lunch and saw immediately that there was turmoil in the dispatch room.

"What's going on?" asked Lenina.

"And what's a one eight seven?"

Lenina shrugged and punched up the information on the nearest terminal.

"One eight seven . . ." Lenina was stunned. "That's a murder-death-kill!"

"A *what*!" yelled Garcia.

Lenina managed to keep her head while those around her were losing theirs. She eyed the coordinates on the illuminated map and punched in the proper codes. The chart vanished and was replaced by a liquid crystal display scene of the Cryo-Penitentiary hearing room. Two guards lay still, right where Phoenix had dropped them, and the camera picked up the body of Warden Smithers. He was still alive and crawling for the door.

The socket of his right eye was a gory crater, and blood streamed from the wound onto the polished floor. His ravaged face looked as if it had been put through a meat grinder. The cops observing in the station house had to shield their eyes from such a brutal image.

The computer voice was as placid as always, even in the face of such brutal butchery. "Here reporting two stopped codes at Cryo-Prison X twenty-three dash one," the computer intoned.

The machine scanned for further life codes in the room. "Plus William Smithers, Warden. Severe injury. Do you wish to assign medic?"

Before Lenina could respond with a code on her keyboard, William Smithers stopped crawling, collapsing to the floor. Blood continued to pour from his terrible wound.

"Update," the computer reported. "Specification deceased. Do you wish to assign coroner?"

The eight or ten cops in the room continued to stare at the monitor, mouths open, not quite sure what to do next. Just then Chief Earle strode into the room, exuding an in-charge air, even though he had not the slightest idea what was going on.

"What is the matter with all of you?" he demanded, casting an angry eye over his force.

"Cryo-Prison, sir," Alfredo Garcia managed to stammer. "Three nonsanctioned life terminations. At Cryo Prison X23-1. One of them is the warden."

"What!"

James MacMillan looked as if he was on the verge of tears. "Murder-death-kills, sir," he said, choking back sobs. "Three MDKs."

For a long moment Chief Earle stood absolutely still as his brain tried to process the amazing information he had just received. "I . . . I . . . I think we should—"

"Access the cryo-pen's morning hearing schedule," said Lenina, her hands flying over the keyboard of her computer. "Let's see who the warden was dealing with."

"Yes'. . . yes," sputtered Chief Earle. "Do that."

The rest of the police officers in the room appeared to be in a zombielike trance at the news from the Cryo-Penitentiary. All of them except for Lenina, of course, and an elderly black cop just days away from retirement—a man named Zachary Lamb.

As the parole-hearing schedule came up on Lenina Huxley's vdt screen, Zachary leaned over her shoulder, scanning the information readout.

"All but one prisoner were returned to their cryo pods this morning," Lenina reported. "The missing one is the last the warden was scheduled to see today. The name is . . . Phoenix. Simon Phoenix."

Zach Lamb inhaled sharply. "Simon Phoenix?"

That was a name out of a nightmare—a nightmare he hadn't had since his rookie stint in Hover-Command, back in the old days. A lot had changed since then—not always changes Lamb had approved of. But he had to admit, that it had been a long, long time since a man like Simon Phoenix had walked the streets of Los . . . *San* Angeles. And to Zachary Lamb's way of thinking that was a change for the better.

Lenina half turned in her chair. "You know that name?"

Zachary Lamb nodded gravely. "I knew him. We all knew him back in the old days. He's evil like you've only read about, girl. He's—"

"Hold that thought, Zachary Lamb," said Huxley. She punched some more information into her keyboard. "I want Simon Phoenix's code. Now!"

The computer took only a second to search its huge memory bank. "There are no specifications on file for a Simon Phoenix," reported the unflappable voice.

Huxley almost slapped the side of her monitor. "L-7, you aren't coming down with a virus are you? You have to have a code on Phoenix!"

"You don't get it, Lenina Huxley," said Zach Lamb, shaking his head slowly. "Phoenix isn't coded. He got chilled back in the twentieth, before they started lojacking everybody."

"But you were around then," said Lenina. "You must have some idea who this is."

"I do. Wish I didn't. I was a rookie then. He was a big dealer. Narcotics. Software. Wetware. Prostitution. Loan-sharking. Murder for hire, murder for the fun of it. Anything where he thought he could make a little money. Make himself a bigger man. Simon Phoenix was always behind it. You could bet on it."

Lenina Huxley's mind swam at the thought of such outlandish, flamboyant late twentieth-century crime. It sounded like something out of a fairy tale. And she felt the tiniest tingle of excitement. She was, after all, a romantic at heart.

"Phoenix declared his own kingdom in South Central LA. And he MDKed whatever got in his way. In a bad time, Lenina Huxley, he was the worst."

Huxley's thought of South Central San Angeles, an area of neat, well-kept megabuildings, and couldn't quite picture a private kingdom of crime there in such a docile, quiet, untroubled neighborhood.

Alfredo Garcia was the next to recover from the shock of the horrifying events of the day. He had scanned the area around the prison and had discovered the dead motorist in the penitentiary parking lot. The man lay sprawled on the asphalt, his eyes open but unseeing to the bright blue sky, a very, very surprised look on his face.

Garcia immediately queried the mainframe for a report.

"One stopped code in penitentiary parking area," the voice reported without emotion. John Mostow, doctor."

More wails and sobs came from the assembled policemen. This latest fatality brought the body count up to four people dead in a matter of minutes—more murders than had been committed in the city in the last three decades. Merwin, in particular, was beside himself with grief, and his weeping was beginning to get on Lenina's nerves. She gave his rolling chair a firm push, sending the distraught man drifting away across the station.

Huxley turned back to her computer. "Is the doctor's conveyance still in the parking zone?"

The reply was instantaneous. "The doctor's vehicle has been code fixed approaching the corner of Wilshire and Santa Monica Boulevard."

Lenina Huxley pounded her fist in delight. "Glorious!"

Chief Earle was beginning to recover and reasserted his command. "Fine work, Huxley. Order all nearby units. ProtecServe Wilshire and Santa Monica."

Alfredo Garcia beamed at his partner. "Is there

anything more groovy than the prevailing of justice?''

Lenina Huxley could feel the adrenaline surge in the room as the San Angeles Police Force sprang into action. Even Merwin and MacMillan were wiping away their tears, comforted by knowing that justice would be done.

Of course no man or woman in the room had even dreamed of the day they would hear of murder being committed in the city of San Angeles.

7

When Phoenix saw the rotating, speaking street sign that marked the corner of Wilshire and Santa Monica, he brought his car to a halt and jumped out, looking around the famous intersection for something he recognized. The Beverly Hilton was gone, that weird-looking CAA building was gone . . . The Wilson's House of Suede and Leather was still there, a testament to the continuum of history. Phoenix sighed in relief—at least something never changed.

On one corner there was something he had never seen before, but which, curiously, something at the back of his mind told him to look for. It was a CompuKiosk, the twenty-first century's answer to the lowly phone both.

A CompuKiosk *did* contain a telephone, but it

had much more. It was a full-service computer access center that provided all manner of assistance to San Angelenos. With a row of large buttons, a monitor, and a keyboard, all it took was the right set of codes to dial up all kinds of information.

Right then the booth was occupied by a troubled-looking fellow who was sadly pouring his heart out to the computer terminal.

"I dunno . . . Lately I just don't feel like there's anything special about me . . ."

The computer's voice was male this time, but its tone was just as reassuring as its female counterpart.

"You are an incredibly sensitive person," it told the upset young man soothingly, "and you inspire joy-joy feelings in all those around you . . ."

The fellow seemed to brighten slightly. "Really? Then why is it I always feel so . . . so . . ."

He never got the chance to pose his question because Simon Phoenix had reached into the booth and yanked him out, throwing him roughly aside.

"Get lost, jerk," he ordered. The man, who already had trouble with his self-esteem, slunk away, his feelings of inadequacy confirmed.

Phoenix turned his attention to the booth and examined the array of services the CompuKiosk offered. There were buttons marked ego boost, citizen confessional, public psychiatrist, atlas, serenity sayings, banking, mail, telephone directory, and information.

Just for the hell of it, Simon Phoenix hit the ego boost button.

"You look great today," said the computer voice.

Simon grinned. "Thanks, feel great, too."

"You inspire love and loyalty in your family and associates," the computer continued, laying on the flattery with an electronic trowel.

"How true," said Phoenix, laughing. The future amused the hell out of him. But he didn't need his ego stroked anymore. He hit the information button and then dropped his hands onto the keyboard, plugging into the information net as fast as he could.

A different computer voice answered his queries. "You have reached secure mailbox facilities for— Simon Phoenix."

He cackled. "Hey! That's me! Tell me what's up!" Information began flashing on the screen. Edgar Friendly's photograph was the first up, followed by the Scraps leader's life story; then maps of the city, routes, overhead and underground plans of the city.

Phoenix took it all in just by staring at the screen, soaking up the information like a huge human sponge. The data flew by at light speed, but the velocity did not faze Simon Phoenix for a moment.

"Damn, I'm possessed!" he said amazed at his own dexterity with the computer. "I wonder if I can play the accordion now, too."

The information continued to blast across the screen. "Keep it comin', that's it. That's good." The screen told him everything he needed to know—except one thing. Phoenix pounced on the keyboard and played a computer concerto, pulling up the information he *really* wanted.

"Gun," he whispered. "Tell me about guns, Mr. Wizard. Where to get 'em."

The computer voice was, this time, like a narrator in a nature documentary.

"Noun: gun. Portable firearm. This device was widely utilized in the urban wars of the late twentieth century. Referred to as a gun, a pistol, piece, heat—"

"I know all that!" yelled Simon Phoenix. "I don't want a history lesson. *Hal*! Tell me where I can get hold of some goddamn guns!"

A morality box on the wall of the CompuKiosk buzzed into life. "You are fined one credit violation of the verbal morality statute." A thin sheet of paper slid out of the box, the reprimand printed in red on one side. Phoenix snatched the piece of paper, balled it up and tossed it away.

"Yeah?" said Simon Phoenix. "Well fuck you two times."

The box buzzed twice and two more sheets of paper appeared. The voice was very stern this time. "Your repeated violation of the verbal morality statute has caused me to notify the San Angeles Police Department. Please remain in place for your reprimand."

"Is that a fact?" He was just about to punch out the box when two SAPD cruisers screeched to a halt right in front of him.

"Oooh," said Phoenix. "You fuckers are fast, too." Before the morality box could pipe up, Phoenix buzzed at it himself—and punched in the speaker.

Four cops stood in the middle of the intersection. They were dressed in the standard patrol garb of the San Angeles Police Department—blue tunics over blue riding breeches, a Sam Browne belt across the chest, and tall black side-buckle boots. Strapped to their waists were long scabbards that looked as if they contained thick swords.

Phoenix took a step forward and folded his arms. "Now, don't you fellows look sharp!"

In unison the four police officers unsheathed the electronic stun batons they carried in the leather cases. The batons hummed slightly when they were switched on.

Phoenix was not aware of it, but a camera at the top of one of the light stanchions by the side of the boulevard swiveled and focused on him, beaming pictures of the encounter back to Lenina Huxley's station where the images were flashed on the giant screen in the dispatch room.

As the street cops began moving in on Phoenix, the cops in the station began to clap and cheer.

"Chalk one up for the actions of the benevolent ones," said Alfredo Garcia.

Another squad car screeched to a halt and two more policemen emerged, one of them the sector squad leader. He got in position, glancing nervously at the Strategic Apprehension Computer he carried in his hand.

"Maniac is imminent," said the squad leader to the screen. "Request advice."

The computer did not hesitate. "In a firm tone of voice, demand maniac lie down with hands behind back."

The squad leader nodded. "Simon Phoenix," he shouted, "lie down and put your hands behind your back."

Simon guffawed loudly and slapped his hip. "Geez, gosh. Six of you. And in such tidy uniforms, too. I'm so scared."

The police looked puzzled. "If you are scared," suggested the squad leader, "you should surrender immediately."

Phoenix shook his head. "Don't you guys have a sense of irony anymore?" Turning his back on the policemen, he returned to the terminal and started typing busily.

The squad leader sounded distinctly hurt and aggrieved. "Maniac has responded with mocking laughter and words," he reported to the Strategic Apprehension Computer, like a little boy tattling on a bully.

"Approach and repeat the ultimatum," advised the SAC computer, "but use a firmer tone of voice . . . and add the words, 'or else.'"

The squad leader cleared his throat. "Simon Phoenix, lie down on the ground, or else."

Phoenix typed a code into the computer, and the graffiti-removing shock poles sprung from the kiosk sides, but instead of zapping a slogan off the wall, the bars swooped down on the nearest cop and electrocuted him. He jerked and sizzled as the juice zapped through him, his hair crackling and burning. It took less than three seconds to kill him. The whole area was suddenly filled with the smell of cooked meat and smoldering cloth.

The cops on the scene and the cops watching on the monitor were stunned.

"Attack!" ordered the Strategic Apprehension Computer.

The members of the SAPD were nothing if not brave. The three cops closest to Simon Phoenix moved in, swinging their stun batons for all they were worth, trying to take out "the maniac" with a single blow. If they could just touch Simon Phoenix with the rods, they *would* be able to apprehend him—not even he would have been able to withstand the short, sharp, shock of electricity.

Of course they never stood a chance. Simon Phoenix waded into the two men quickly. With the hard edge of his right hand, he snapped a neck, sending the nearest cop dropping to the pavement, his head lolling to one side at an odd and unnatural angle.

Next he wheeled and speared-handed another policeman, jamming his rigid fingers into the sternum, driving fragments of ribs into the heart of his next victim. The bone chips were as hard as bullets. The ripped heart stopped midbeat.

Phoenix turned to the third and with a well-placed foot, kicked the third cop violently in the chin, driving the man's jawbone straight up and into the brain.

The last two cops were terrified and had not the slightest idea what to do. Even the Strategic Apprehension Computer was silent on the subject.

Phoenix turned and swaggered forward. "And then there were two . . .''

The policemen started to back away as Simon Phoenix advanced on them.

"Hey! I'm new in town . . . This is no way to treat a stranger. Not nice." He wagged a finger at the two completely petrified men.

That was all it took. The two cops knew they had to get out of there in a hurry. They turned and started running down Wilshire toward Beverly Hills.

Phoenix vaulted up and over the police car, effortlessly catching up with the two men. He stopped in front of them, corraling them like a sheepdog.

"You know . . . I hate rejection. It just doesn't sit well with me. Makes me upset. And when I get upset . . ." His actions spoke louder than his words.

He fell on one of the cops and kicked him hard in the throat, shattering his larynx. The man dropped to the ground, and Phoenix kicked his head into the curbstone, as if he was place kicking a football. The cop's head split open like a watermelon, blood gushing down the street and into the storm drain.

The last was the squad leader. Phoenix walked up to him, pulled the computer from his hands, dropped it, and stepped on it, grinding the machine into dust.

His response was purely instinctual. "That's police property," said the appalled squad leader.

"I'm sorry," said Phoenix. He put out both wrists, as if expecting handcuffs. "Here I am, officer. All you have to do is take me in . . ."

But the cop was rooted to the spot, and he stared at Simon Phoenix, transfixed, unable to move, a deer caught in some onrushing headlights.

"Simon says . . . scream!"

Phoenix attacked. He grabbed the squad leader by the shoulders and drove him to the ground, flipping him over on his stomach as he fell. Sitting astride his hapless victim's back, he swatted away the man's hat, grabbed a handful of hair, and viciously smashed his head into the ungiving roadbed.

Time and again Phoenix rocked back and forth, hammering the policeman's head over and over until jaws, teeth, tongue, and eyes were oozing from his skull.

"Well, I think that ought to do it," he said finally. Phoenix stood up. Blood flecked his pants and his hands were stained with gore.

He took a shallow breath and looked around as if wondering what to do next, now that there were no more people in the immediate vicinity that he could kill.

Back in the police station the whole gruesome death ballet had been watched in shocked silence. Now that six—*six!*—San Angeles Police Department operatives lay dead, Merwin began to sob quietly.

Lenina Huxley's blood seemed to burn in her veins. She had never seen anything even remotely as horrible as the terrible scene that had unfolded before her eyes.

Simon Phoenix finally spotted the security camera that had recorded the entire bloody incident. A big grin on his face, he strode toward it, swinging a stun baton as if it were a walking stick. He ripped the cover plate from the camera stanchion and peered directly into the lens.

"Simon says stand!"

In fear and confusion half of the cops in the dispatch room actually did stand. Lenina Huxley didn't. She just stared at the huge, grotesque closeup of Phoenix on the monitor. It was a face she would never forget.

Oddly enough, the next thing Phoenix did was begin to sing. He did not have a very good voice, and it took the cops watching his performance a moment or two to realize that he was singing an odd parody of the old national anthem "The Star-Spangled Banner."

Oh-oh say can you see
a bad guy like me?
Who so real-ly wants,
to cause you some trouble.

Who-oo kills just for fun
With his hands or a gun
Or a knife or a bomb
Or a bro-oh-ken bottle.

And I'll make you all sweat
Till you really regret,
The time that you made
me stay in that hell hole.

Oh say can you under-er-stand
just what I am saying?
Here in the laaand of
fear and the home of the
    slaves.

When Simon Phoenix had finished singing his little ditty, he grinned as if he was very pleased with himself, and then peered deep into the camera lens. Lenina Huxley shivered a little, as if he was looking directly at her, taunting and mocking her with his one blue and his one brown eye.

"Play ball," he said ominously. Then he jammed the stun baton into the transmission cables and the picture shorted out. A cloud of static filled the screen.

8

It took a moment or two for the cops in the station to react to this bizarre performance. Lenina Huxley was first to snap out of the hypnotic effects of the senseless violence, and she realized that it was essential to keep in visual contact with Simon Phoenix. Her nimble fingers danced over her computer console, trying to bring up the optic net that encircled the Wilshire–Santa Monica intersection.

But Simon Phoenix's action had blown the electrical currents all over the neighborhood.

"We've lost every camera for six blocks in every direction," she announced. Plainly, Lenina Huxley was thinking fast. "I'm going to Century City at twelve hundred millimeters."

She punched up a few more codes, opening up a huge lensed camera mounted on the roof of the old

Century Plaza Hotel in the complex called Century City.

The camera picked him up quickly enough. He was under the hood of one of the SAPD cruisers, jamming at something with his stun baton.

Finally, Lenina was stumped. "What is he doing?"

Alfredo Garcia supplied the answer, "He's going for the vehicle battery core. The capitance gel is what he's after, I'll bet."

"Why on earth is he doing that?" asked James MacMillan between sobs.

The answer was not long in coming. Evidently, Simon Phoenix found what he was looking for. He backed away from the car quickly, getting well out of range just in time. A second later the car exploded in a great gout of smoke and flame.

By the time the billowing smoke cleared, Simon Phoenix had vanished. There was dead silence in the room as the policemen watched the car burning merrily.

"Goddammit!" shouted Lenina. Of course, that single word was followed by the predictable buzz of the morality box. Some things never changed . . .

The man who had created San Angeles—and now the absolute ruler of the city under the title of Mayor-Gov—was Dr. Raymond Cocteau. He was the architect of the order that governed the lives of every San Angeleno, and while he held a title that suggested some form of democracy, Dr. Cocteau was, in fact, elected for life. His power was absolute and unquestioned—except for the few Scraps who chose to attach themselves to Edgar Friendly.

Despite Dr. Cocteau's supreme power, the Mayor-Gov was obsessed by the thought of Edgar Friendly and his ragtag band of followers. The Scraps so consumed him that he was apt to give lengthy lectures to the eight-person San Angeles Board of Supervisors, who were officials directly under Cocteau and who were responsible for carrying out his orders quickly and to the letter.

The eight supervisors were powerful people, and they lived far better than the rest of the population. The boring harangues from their illustrious leader was one major drawback to a job that promised great wealth and power.

The instant Cocteau had been informed of the graffiti incident, the Mayor-Gov had convened a meeting of his supervisory board, the topic once again, predictably, the need to eradicate Edgar Friendly and the Scraps.

There were eight video screens arranged in a row in front of Dr. Raymond Cocteau's vast desk, each one marked with a sign that denoted the area of responsibility of each. The eight city departments were Orderly Conduct, Morality, Waste Management, Power Grid, Consumption, Transport, Sanitation and Health, and Habitation. The eight supervisors on the screens listened attentively to their illustrious leader.

"The problem," said Cocteau, "is not just the defacement of public buildings. And the problem is not the noise pollution of the exploding devices." The Mayor-Gov always spoke in a low, controlled and supremely reasonable tone of voice.

"Allow me to explain," Dr Cocteau continued.

"The real problem lies in the man whose initials mark the detonating graffiti, Edgar Friendly."

At the mention of the name, the eight supervisors grumbled unhappily.

"For a sadly extended period of time," said Cocteau, "we in San Angeles have been plagued by packs of subterranean hooligans—the Scraps as they are known—a collection of men and women who left the comfort of our society only to spew hostility at the very bosom they have relinquished."

"Disgraceful," said the supervisor in charge of Orderly Conduct. He had reason to feel a little hot under the collar—after all, elimination of the Scraps did fall under the umbrella of his department.

Dr. Cocteau ignored the man and continued speaking. "There was a time when we thought of these Scraps as pathetic and relatively harmless. Now they have a leader. Edgar Friendly seems to be relentless in his ambition to infect our harmony with his venom. He must, of course, be stopped."

"Absolutely," agreed the supervisor of Waste Management.

Dr. Cocteau paused for a moment as if wondering how much his commissioners needed to know.

"Forty years ago," Cocteau continued, "forty years ago when Los Angeles exploded in violenceAnger, violenceHatred, and violenceFear, a disease had erupted . . . A disease not socioeconomic, but *behavioral*."

There was a round of nods from the eight supervisors. Of course no one ever disagreed with the Mayor-Gov.

"People had simply forgotten how to behave,"

said Cocteau. "And we simply cannot allow it again."

"Never," said the supervisor of Sanitation and Health, who was understandably touchy on the subject of disease—any kind of disease, even a behavioral one.

"In former times, politics, law, even force were useless to affect change . . . We have triumphed over all of that. The same principals of B.E., Behavioral Engineering, I have applied to the cryo prisons were expanded into the design and execution of what we now call"—Dr. Cocteau gestured expansively and he beamed with pride—"San Angeles. It is a city as fine as any of the holding facilities I have designed. We have a peacefulSafe and above all a happy-happy population."

The head supervisors nodded and muttered their heartfelt approval.

"This radical terrorist behavior inspired by Edgar Friendly must not be allowed to threaten our safety. Our motto must be Safety Above All."

"Hear hear," said the supervisors with great spirit.

Cocteau held up his hands to quiet them. "Even now I am positing actions and postulating proceedings that will abate this threat to our city's stability. I expect your trustConfidence and certitude."

"As always, Mayor-Gov Raymond Cocteau," said Waste Management, speaking for all of the supervisors.

Cocteau's assistant, Associate Bob, slipped into the Mayor-Gov's office and gave his master a significant look, as if he had some urgent information.

"If you will excuse me," said Cocteau to the

monitors. He waved dismissively, and suddenly, the sound muted and the images of the supervisors froze.

Bob crossed to Cocteau, his head down obsequiously. Bob was a large man with an oddly high-pitched voice for a man his size. He had the remarkable ability to appear fawning and officious at the same time.

"Mayor-Gov Raymond Cocteau," he said, "a cryo-con has effected self-release from the cryo-penitentiary." Associate Bob appeared quite shaken by the news. "It is quite horrific. A number of murder-death-kills. All manner of categories of chaos." Bob shuddered at the thought.

"Enhance your calm, Associate Bob," said Dr. Cocteau soothingly. "Enhance your calm . . ."

"I apologize, Mayor-Gov Raymond Cocteau."

"Don't concern yourself." Dr. Cocteau gestured toward the heads frozen on the video screen. "Be well then for me. And get Chief George Earle immediately."

"Yes, Mayor-Gov. Without delay."

Chief Earle had been expecting the summons from the Mayor-Gov, but he was still shaken by Simon Phoenix's savage disregard for human life.

"It was just . . . I mean it was so . . . just so graphic," the police chief stammered via his video screen. "How a man could be so glibly sadistic . . . It was fun for him. He was amused by it all."

Cocteau nodded. "I want you to do everything in your power to snare this agent of destruction. Do you understand, George Earle? You have my utmost confidence."

"Yes, Mayor-Gov."

"Utmost confidence. Be well." Mayor-Gov Cocteau clicked off the screen.

Chief Earle stood in the middle of the dispatch room and looked at his assembled policemen. He looked as if he were completely flummoxed by his assignment. There was silence in the station, no one knowing quite what to say. Lenina rested her head in her hands, still in shock over what she had witnessed.

Chief Earle seemed on the verge of tears. "That maniac murder-death-killed every man in a six-member squad. And *they* had a Strategic Apprehension Computer. He destroyed an official vehicle. Mayor-Gov Raymond Cocteau recommends we use everything in our power—but what else is there?"

Nobody could answer his question. The cops in the room all looked down at their shoes or out the window, anything to avoid Chief Earle's eyes. They looked like schoolboys surprised by a pop quiz. But Lenina Huxley did not appear to be baffled. She looked up suddenly.

"Zachary Lamb! How did they apprehend this fiendish Simon Phoenix back in the twentieth?" she asked.

Zachary Lamb sighed heavily, as if not wanting to remember those bad old days. "There was a twelve-state manhunt, even satellite surveillance," he said. "They devoted a whole show to Simon Phoenix on *Unsolved Mysteries* . . ."

"And?" asked Lenina Huxley.

"And none of it worked," said Lamb. "In the end it took one man. One cop. John Spartan."

Lenina's eyes brightened. "John Spartan? You mean the Demolition Man?" she asked.

9

Lenina Huxley knew just where to look for more information on John Spartan, a.k.a. the Demolition Man. Everything anyone needed to know was right there in the police computer. She summoned up his video file, and Chief Earle, Garcia, and Lamb hunched over Huxley's video console, watching as the compilation of ancient news clips and police video tape showed highlights of Spartan's colorful career.

There was shot after shot of Spartan dragging prisoners from destroyed buildings or rescuing hostages from fiery infernos. It was a nonstop collection of explosions, firefights, and blasts, a montage of devastated buildings and dead bad guys. But the one thing that bound all of the incidents together was the final result—John Spartan always got his man.

Lenina's eyes glowed as she watched, feeling a tingle of excitement every time Spartan once again vanquished one of society's enemies. Things might have been dangerous and dirty in the bad old days, but no one could deny that it was quite thrilling.

"Are you sure this is real life?" asked Garcia. He couldn't quite believe what he was seeing.

"Barely," said Huxley. "Spartan is a legend."

"How do you know so much about him, Lenina Huxley?" demanded Chief Earle.

"I did a historical study on him last year, which I guess none of you perused. Spartan made one thousand arrest in three years. All authentic criminals."

"There was a lot more business back then," said Lamb. "More business than we could handle."

Lenina was still transfixed by the screen. "Watch this," she said. "This is my favorite . . . Spartan has been called in to effect a hostage rescue."

John Spartan could be seen on the grainy video tape, walking away from a complex of buildings that were being engulfed in flame. He had a young girl slung over his shoulder like a sack of potatoes.

A TV camera crew came scrambling over to the cop and thrust a microphone into his face. A female reporter had to yell her question to make herself heard over the sounds of explosions in the background. "How can you justify destroying a seven-million-dollar minimall to rescue a girl whose ransom was only twenty-five thousand dollars?"

"Drop dead, lady!" squealed the little girl.

"Good answer," growled Spartan.

"Such rudeness," said Garcia.

But Lenina was smiling, captivated by the images unfolding on her screen. In contrast, Chief Earle was aghast. He shook his head and turned away from the video display terminal.

"This is a recommendation?" he asked in disbelief. "Lenina Huxley, your Demolition Man is an animal!"

Huxley did not disagree, not exactly. "He is clearly the man for a job such as this. Chief Earle, you have the authority to reinstate him."

Zachary Lamb agreed. "Simon Phoenix is an old-fashioned criminal. We need an old-fashioned cop to deal with him."

Earle shook his head. "He is a muscle-bound grotesque who hasn't worn a shield in forty years."

"But this guy must be over seventy years old," put in Alfredo Garcia.

Lenina Huxley beamed. "That's the joy-joy part of all this," she said. "John Spartan hasn't aged a day since he put Simon Phoenix away back in 1993."

"What does *that* mean, Lenina Huxley," demanded Chief Earle. "Explain yourself."

Huxley smiled mischievously. "John Spartan is himself a cryo-con . . ."

The status panel next to John Spartan's cryo-cell had not changed its reading in thirty-six years. *Cellular Activity*: Null. *Temperature*: .5 Degree Kelvin. As the autolock began to unwind, the cryo-cell rose from the floor of the prison, revealing the inert form of John Spartan. He hadn't moved, breathed, hadn't so much as blinked in three and a half decades.

Two technician-operators wearing insulated suits and gloves moved in. One man fired up a magnesium thermite laser, a hand-held machine about the size of a skill saw. The other technician maneuvered a crane with a three-clawed arm into position and seized the cell and moved it into the defrosting chamber.

It took seven hours to thaw out John Spartan, a gradual process that required great skill and precision. If done too fast there would be serious brain and cell damage; if executed too slowly then the prisoner ran the risk of dying a very slow death from lack of oxygen.

However, in Spartan's case the warming-up process was successful, and in a matter of hours Spartan, still semicomatose, was hustled into a conference room where Lenina Huxley, Chief Earle, and Alfredo Garcia were waiting for him.

Spartan was wearing an industrial gray jumpsuit, and he sat slumped in his seat, trying with little success to focus on the room around him. He hadn't taken in exactly what had happened to him or where he was; he couldn't even get a fix on the sealed cryo-package containing his personal effects that lay in the middle of the table.

"Hunting down an escaped cryo-con by releasing another one," harrumphed Earle, shaking his head. "I am unconvinced. And what would Mayor-Gov Raymond Cocteau say!"

"This is within the power of the police charter, sir," said Lenina Huxley quickly. "He can be released on limited parole and reinstated to active duty.''

Her partner, Alfredo Garcia, wasn't convinced either. ''It's not enough for you to collect the twentieth, Lenina Huxley. You have to bring them back to life.''

''Dr. Cocteau said we must use everything in our power,'' Huxley retorted. ''I still can't think of a better idea for subjugating the maniac.''

Earle folded his arms across his chest. ''That still doesn't mean that this is a good idea, Lenina Huxley. This man comes from a dissimilar method of law enforcement.'' He peered at the quasicatatonic figure. ''I'm not sure he's any different from Simon Phoenix himself.''

Spartan heard the name and jumped as if he had been shocked. He opened his eyes and stared at the two men and the woman and then looked around, as if looking for danger. He tried to stand, but his legs were rubbery and unsteady. He sank back down into the seat and pointed at Garcia.

''You . . .'' His voice was scratchy and rasping.

Garcia gulped. ''Me?''

Spartan clawed his arm. ''Where am I?''

Garcia glanced at his colleagues, unsure of how to answer John Spartan. ''Uh . . . I . . . Uh?''

Spartan pushed Garcia away. ''*When* am I?''

Garcia licked his lips nervously. ''Uh, it's Thursday. Tomorrow is Arbor Day . . .'' He realized he should tell Spartan the truth. ''And last week you turned seventy-four years old. Happy birthday.''

Spartan's eyes opened wider, as if he was finally emerging from a deep sleep. ''What?''

Lenina Huxley decided that it was time to be a

little more businesslike. She spoke clearly and concisely. "Detective, I'm Lieutenant Lenina Huxley. The year is 2032. The reason you have been released—"

Spartan was shaking off his grogginess quickly now. "How long have I been under," he demanded.

"Thirty-six years," said Lenina Huxley matter-of-factly.

"Whoa," said Spartan. Suddenly he felt weak again, and he slumped in his chair.

"Now listen, Spartan—" said Earle officiously.

"I had a wife," said Spartan interrupting. "Where is she? What happened to my wife?"

Huxley had anticipated this question. "Your wife's light was extinguished in the Big One of 2010," she said briskly.

"Her what? When?"

"Uh, she died. In an earthquake. In *the* earthquake. Twenty-two years ago."

This piece of information stabbed deep into Spartan's heart, and it took several moments for it to sink in. Then he spoke haltingly.

"My wife and I, we had a little girl. A daughter . . ." It was all coming back to him now. "I made her a promise. What happened to her?"

"John Spartan," said Earle, trying again to assert his authority. "I am Chief of Police George Earle. We did not thaw you out for a family reunion. It is fortunate the lieutenant took the time to research the whereabouts of your wife. The reason for your reactivation is the cryo-con Simon Phoenix."

"What are you talking about? He got more time than I did. He should still be here, on ice."

Huxley stepped in. "This morning Simon Phoenix escaped from this cryo-facility. We have had ten murder-death-kills so far. We have become a society of peace, loving, and understanding. And we are, quite frankly, not equipped to deal with this kind of situation.''

John Spartan was staring at the pretty young woman as if she had lost her mind.

Alfredo Garcia tried to put things in perspective. "There have been no deaths through unnatural causes in San Angeles in the last sixteen years," he said.

"In where?"

"The Santa Barbara/Los Angeles/San Diego Metroplex merged in 2011," Huxley explained. "You are in the center of what used to be called Los Angeles."

It took a moment for Spartan to absorb this piece of amazing information. "Great. That's great . . ." He wiped his hand across his face and decided first things first. He had a thirty-six-year appetite and thirst to boot. "God, I'm so hungry. I'd kill for a burrito . . ."

The three police officers recoiled in fear.

"Kill?" said Alfredo Garcia uneasily. In the past, he knew people did get killed for the most trivial of reasons.

"It's just an expression," Spartan explained. "Don't worry about it." His throat was dry and his skin itched. He scratched the back of his hand vigorously. He had noticed that there was a small incision in the skin. "Okay. Try this. Go get me a Bud."

Garcia smiled ingratiatingly. "Of course. Right away. But what is a Bud?"

Spartan grimaced. "A beer." He gave up on brand loyalty. "It doesn't have to be a Bud. A beer, any beer."

The three cops looked horrified.

"Alcohol is not good for you," said Lenina Huxley sternly.

"It's not supposed to be good for you," snapped John Spartan. "It's supposed to make you feel better. Or not feel anything, depending on the dosage."

Huxley was not amused. "It has been deemed that everything that is not good for you is bad. Hence—illegal. Cigarettes, caffeine, contact sports, meat . . ."

This was about as weird as it got. Spartan gaped. "You have got to be shittin' me!"

But then things got weirder.

The omnipresent morality box buzzed into life. "John Spartan, you are fined one credit for a violation of verbal morality statute 113."

Spartan stared as the slip of paper wound out of the morality box. "What the hell is that?"

The morality box droned again, oblivious to Spartan's disbelieving gaze. "John Spartan, you are fined one credit for a violation of verbal morality statute 113."

"Bad language, chocolate, gasoline, uneducational toys, and anything spicy—all have been deemed illegal," Lenina Huxley continued. "Abortion is also illegal, but then again, so is pregnancy if you don't have a license."

"This is crazy," said Spartan. He wondered if this was all some kind of nightmare. But in thirty-six years, he hadn't one. This, he concluded, must be real life. John Spartan didn't like it.

Chief Earle was getting impatient with all this talk. He had a direct command from Mayor-Gov Raymond Cocteau himself—not something to take lightly.

"Caveman, let us finish all the Rip Van Winkle stuff and get on with the business at hand. A Mr. Simon Phoenix has risen from the ashes. You have been brought out of cryo suspension to help in the apprehension of this criminal."

It was well in the past, but John Spartan remembered what happened to him the last time he nailed Simon Phoenix. He shook his head abruptly. "Uh huh. No way. I tracked that dirtbag for two years, and when I finally brought him down, they turned me into an ice cube for my trouble." He shrugged. "Thanks, but no thanks. Not this time. I learn from my mistakes."

Chief Earle stood his ground. "The conditions of your parole are full reinstatement into the San Angeles Police Department and immediate assignment to the apprehension of Simon Phoenix. Or you can go back into cryo-stasis."

Involuntarily, Spartan shuddered, remembering the freezer. It had been bad—way bad. He would never go back to that, not if he could avoid it.

Lenina Huxley leaned forward and looked into his eyes. "Not many people get a second chance, John Spartan."

1 0

Newly fitted out in his SAPD uniform, John Spartan looked like a spit-and-polish police officer of the twenty-first century. He felt like a buffoon.

Standing in front of Lenina Huxley's police car, Spartan examined the uniform, from the cute little cap down to his side-buckled knee boots.

"What am I supposed to be? A drum major?" he said in disgust. "This isn't a cop uniform. This is a joke. What am I going to do? Lead the Rose Bowl parade?" He slapped his pockets and rattled his equipment belt. "What *is* all this stuff?"

Huxley pointed to each piece of hardware as she spoke. "Direct biolink readouts for vitals," she said. "VOX radio contact, base and inter officer coded by rank, partner status, and case priority. Got it?"

Spartan pointed to one more piece of equipment, a thin silver instrument about four inches in length. "What's that?"

"Your whistle. It goes in your breast pocket."

God save me, thought Spartan.

"You have to have a whistle," said Garcia earnestly.

"Of course," he said. "That's great. In case one of the floats gets loose, I can direct traffic."

"Traffic difficulties have been largely eliminated," said Lenina Huxley.

"You can call it San Angeles or Los Angeles," said John Spartan skeptically, "but there are always traffic jams in southern California."

Lenina Huxley smiled smugly. "If you get in my vehicle, I will demonstrate."

Spartan jammed himself into the back of the small automobile and stared out the window, amazed at the shining, clean city populated by happy people. The effects of the freezing were wearing off rapidly, but the skin on the back of his left hand continued to itch, and he scratched at the scab absently as he gazed at the strange new world around him.

"This probably seems quasi strange to you," said Alfredo Garcia.

Spartan laughed shortly. "Quasi strange? This isn't my city. How do you expect me to protect it? I don't understand you people, let alone like you . . ."

Lenina Huxley wasn't going to stand for that. "You come from a society in which the average eighteen-year-old witnessed two hundred thousand acts of simulated violence."

"Yeah," said Spartan, "so?"

"In our society the number would be three or four. If one of these people"—she gestured toward some of the pedestrians on the sidewalk in what Spartan thought must be Westwood—"if they were to see the Three Stooge Men and see the Moe-person hammer the Curly person, they would weep, John Spartan. Weep."

"The Three Stooge Men?" asked John Spartan.

"Myself," said Huxley, "I'm a bit of an aficionado of the shocking, both real and fictional."

"Is that so?"

Huxley nodded. "Like the time you wow-fully tractor-pulled the Santa Monica pier into a heap of rubble in order to snare the team of hit men who—" Lenina was bubbling happily, enthralled by Spartan's past exploits.

But John Spartan wasn't interested in rehashing his old war stories. "I'd like to try to find out what happened to my daughter."

"We have conducted a check of the central personnel computers," said Garcia.

"And your daughter was not present on the city population records," said Lenina Huxley. "We will continue to investigate, but there were no clues to her current whereabouts."

Spartan sighed and shook his head. He felt estranged and alienated from this weird world—and it did not resemble any of the science fiction of his youth. It was a completely foreign place, as strange as a faraway planet.

Lenina Huxley's heart went out to him. "You seem very much alone, John Spartan."

"You might say that," he said sourly.

"Not everything is that different," said Lenina

Huxley. Perhaps you would like to hear the oldies station.'' She winked, like an adult trying to interest a child. "Oldies, John Spartan?''

Garcia grinned as he snapped on the radio. The car filled with music. To Spartan's immense surprise, the "oldies" weren't old songs, but old commercial jingles. In this case, the old Alka-Seltzer song.

Plop-plop, fizz-fizz . . . Oh what a relief it is!
Plop-plop, fizz-fizz . . . Oh what a reliiiiief it is!

"I don't believe it!'' said Spartan.

"This is the most popular station in town,'' Garcia explained. "Nonstop wall-to-wall minitunes. In your day you called them commercials.''

"I knew that,'' said Spartan.

The Alka-Seltzer jingle came to an end, and the supercheery voice of the radio disc jockey broke in. "Coming up in the next half hour, we'll be coming at ya with some more cool minitunes, including some of your big favorites—we'll be hearing The Rotor Rooter song, Coca-Cola and its classic 'I'd Like to Teach the World to Sing,' and the timeless, 'Looks Like a Dress Shoe, Feels Like a Sneaker . . .' But right now here's the number one request of the day, the time-honored jingle for fatty meat tubes—Armour Hot Dogs!''

"Wow,'' said Garcia, "this is my fave!''

"What kind of kids love Armour hot dogs?'' sang the jinglers. "Fat kids, skinny kids, kids who climb on rocks. Tough kids, sissy kids . . .''

Lenina Huxley and Alfredo Garcia sang along, harmonizing with the commercial.

"Even kids with chicken pox love hot dogs, Armour hot dogs. The dogs . . . kids . . . love to bite!"

Spartan scratched and shook his head. "Somebody put me back in the fridge."

Every cop in the central police station had turned out to see John Spartan, the killer cop from a violent past. They were disappointed when only Alfredo Garcia and Lenina Huxley entered the station dispatch room.

"Any new inforama on Simon Phoenix?" asked Lenina, walking up to John MacMillan. They exchanged the nontouching circular hand shake.

MacMillan shook his head. "None . . . So where is the famous John Spartan."

"He went to the bathroom," said Alfredo Garcia with a grin. "I guess he got all thawed out."

The nearest morality box burped a little, not sure if Garcia had made an off-color remark or not.

Spartan emerged from the bathroom and marched through the throng of assembled cops. They stared at him and he stared back—it was hard to imagine who was more freaked out.

MacMillan summoned all his courage and walked up to Spartan, raising his hand to make the nontouching circular hand shake. "John Spartan," said MacMillan, "I formally convey my presence to you."

"Hi," said Spartan. He reached out and shook the tough-looking cop's hand. MacMillan tried not to react, but it was plain that he was repulsed by the skin-to-skin contact. He was disgusted, as if Spartan had spit on him. The entire crowd of cops watching looked horrified by what they had witnessed.

Spartan could see that something was wrong, but he couldn't begin to figure out what it was. Swiftly, Lenina Huxley came to his rescue.

"Ah, John Spartan, we're not used to greetings that involve physical contact."

"Oh," he said. "Thanks for telling me . . ." But there was something else on his mind. "Hey, did you guys know that you're out of toilet paper?"

Garcia looked puzzled. "Toilet paper?"

Lenina Huxley fought down a giggle. "Back in the twentieth," she said, "they used a handful of wadded paper when they had to . . . when they used the bathroom."

"Paper!" said Garcia. The entire squad room roared with laughter. But Spartan was unamused. He had to *go*.

"I'm happy you're happy," he said. "But in the place where the toilet paper is supposed to be, you have a shelf with three little seashells on it."

Merwin, the dispatcher, snickered. "I mean, there were three, right?"

Spartan shot the man a withering glance. "What is that supposed to mean?"

Merwin shrank back, scared to death. "I can see how that would be confusing."

But Spartan was no longer paying attention. He had looked across the room and had spotted an old and familiar face. Zachary Lamb was making his way toward his old friend. Of course Lamb was ancient and Spartan had not aged a day.

"Zach Lamb!" shouted Spartan. "What happened to you?"

Lamb shrugged. "I got old, Spartan. It happens every day. I been grounded—finally."

Spartan could not believe his eyes. "Shit, the last time I saw you, you were nothing more than a punk-assed rook."

The morality box buzzed dutifully. "John Spartan," it announced, "you are fined two credits for a violation of verbal morality statute 113." Two sheets of papers zipped out of the machine. Spartan looked at it and then turned away.

"This is one strange place, Zach."

Lamb laughed. "Ain't this whole setup a mother?"

Garcia and Lenina Huxley were watching the two men closely, like anthropologists observing a strange and primitive tribe.

"They seem to be friends," said Garcia, "yet they speak to each other in the most profane manner."

Lenina Huxley looked annoyed. "If you ever read my research, Alfredo Garcia, you would know that this is the way insecure heterosexual males used to bond."

"Your wife still good-looking?" asked Spartan, elbowing his old friend in the ribs. "She was hot!"

Lamb cackled. "Yeah, well, she may be a hundred and twenty-six, Spartan, but she's still the hottest looking piece of . . . Never mind."

"Go on," said Spartan. "Say it."

"Can't." Lamb shook his head. "I miss the old days . . . But I don't miss Simon Phoenix. You gonna help us nail that son of a . . ."

Spartan shook his head. "I hate reruns," he said. "Seems like this is the first crime you guys have had in a while. All this high-tech stuff and you can't nail him?''

"Not so far."

"Well, I'll help, but first I have business to take care of. Understand?" He grinned at his old friend and walked over to the morality box.

"Shit, fuck, piss, crap, damn, bitch, damn. Fuck." The morality box started buzzing wildly, and it had trouble keeping up with the onslaught of obscenity.

A great long piece of paper scrolled out of the machine. Spartan grabbed it and tore it off. He gathered it up and scrunched it. The paper wadded nicely.

"So much for the three seashells," he said. "I'll be right back."

Lenina had become the de facto investigator of the Simon Phoenix case, and she had convened a conference in her cluttered office.

Simon Phoenix was scratching frantically at the back of his hand. "What is going on here," he asked. "What's the matter with my hand?"

"That's your code," said James MacMillan.

Spartan shot him a look. "My what?"

"Your implanted code," explained Lenina. "Simon Phoenix wasn't coded. But while you were sleeping, you got the chip implanted in your hand. Everyone in the city was installed code. It was the brilliant idea of Dr. Cocteau that an organically bioengineered microchip would be sewn into the skin. Sensors all around the city can zero in on anyone at any time."

James MacMillan shook his head. "I can't even

conceive a visual of what you cops did before it was developed.''

"We worked for a living," said Spartan gruffly. "All this fascist crap makes me want to puke!"

Predictably, the morality box buzzed and began its standard spiel. Everyone in the room ignored it.

Spartan waved his hand at the assembled company. "There's one of those things in me?"

"What do you think you're scratching there, caveman?" demanded Chief Earle. "Did you really think we would let you out without control? Your code was implanted the second you thawed."

Spartan stared angrily at his hand. "Why didn't you just shove a leash up my ass?"

The morality box buzzed. "John Spartan, you have been fined one credit . . .''

Chief Earle was really angry now. "You dirty meat eater! No matter how Viking your era was, I cannot digest how you were ever allowed to wear a badge! I think you're going back to the cryo-pen, John Spartan! How do you like that?"

Lenina Huxley got between the two men. "Could you two please dump some hormones? We need every cortex we can get in this situation."

But Chief Earle was hopping mad. He stormed around the office, shouting at the top of his lungs. Neither Huxley nor Garcia had ever seen their commander so angry.

"We don't need him!" yelled Earle. "Our computer has already examined all feasible scenarios resulting from the appearance of Simon Phoenix, and we have determined he will attempt to start up a new drug lab and form a crime syndicate."

Lenina Huxley's computer chimed in. "That is correct, Chief George Earle," it said smugly.

"Thank you," said Earle, apparently unaware that he was talking to a machine.

Spartan shook his head wearily. "I hate to interrupt you two lovebirds, but that's fucking stupid."

The morality box buzzed into life, of course . . .

"You think he's going to build a business? To serve what market? According to you guys, no one wants drugs in this brave new paradise."

"But it's what he does best!" insisted Earle. "He would naturally follow his inclinations."

Spartan couldn't believe that police work had degenerated so drastically. "Use your heads. Phoenix needs just one thing—a gun. He's going for a gun. Plain and simple."

Spartan raged around the room, and the morality box was having a fit trying to keep up with the ancient cop's offenses.

"Phoenix is a complete megalomaniacal fucking psychopath—"

The box buzzed. "John Spartan, you are fined—"

"Remember, I know this shithead."

The morality box snapped back to the beginning. "John Spartan, you are fined one—"

"And I know that the first thing this motherfucker is going to want to do is wipe those smug fuckin' smiles off your shiny faces—"

"Two . . . Three . . . credits for—"

"Sure," Spartan continued, "he could set up a drug lab, build a market, and handshake your asses to death, but who's got the goddamn patience."

"Four . . . Five . . . credits for violation—"

"Trust me," Spartan concluded. "He's gonna go for a gun. A man like Simon Phoenix *needs* a gun."

"Of verbal morality code 113," the morality box finished breathlessly.

"Preposterous!" yelled Earle. "Nonsense. That is complete bull . . ."

"C'mon," said Spartan. "C'mon. You can do it."

But Chief Earle caught himself in time. "Balderdash," he said. "Who cares what this primate thinks?" He jerked a blunt thumb at Spartan. "Try and resonate some understanding, Spartan. A gun!"

"That's right, Chief, a gun," said John Spartan calmly. "A man like Simon Phoenix feels naked without a gun." Actually, Spartan was feeling a little exposed himself.

"That may be," raged Earle. "But he's out of luck. The only place a person can even view a gun in this city, is at a . . . museum."

"A museum?" said Spartan, thoughtfully. "What museum?"

The San Angeles Museum of Art and History was a vast complex that drew thousands of visitors daily—mostly school groups and boy scout troops who were guided through the exhibits by their history teachers who wanted to reinforce the notion that the bad old days were very bad indeed.

The high-ceilinged rooms contained all manner of artifacts from the dead past, such as the objects in the Hall of Carcinogens, which displayed a collection of cigarettes and cigars, bottles of alcohol, and carefully preserved fatty foods.

The big draw, however, was a model of an old

Los Angeles street—dirty tenement buildings and filthy, violent streets, complete with foul air and coarse, polluted soundtrack.

Visitors clustered around this display, peering at the terrible conditions of the bad old days.

A museum computer box perked up when ever a visitor neared. "If you care to sample what it was like to spend a day in Los Angeles in the twentieth please press button."

Simon Phoenix jammed his thumb into the button. Suddenly, the exhibit exploded in a cacophony of obscene sound. The air in the city street was filled with the noise of honking cars, loud swearing in Spanish, the crack of gunshots, the wail of police sirens, and the abrasive thump of rap music.

A shiver delicious enjoyment ran through Simon Phoenix.

"I *love* it." Then he saw a sign that pointed toward yet another exhibit, the Hall of Violence. He grinned at a passing cub scout. "Home sweet home!"

11

Spartan raced outside to Lenina Huxley's police cruiser, desperate to get to the San Angeles Museum of Art and History before Simon Phoenix managed to arm himself and turn into a *really* dangerous adversary. Lenina and Alfredo Garcia jogged along behind him.

"How can you be sure he went to the museum?" asked Lenina.

"It's a hunch," said Spartan. "Trust me on this. It's a cop thing. Sixth sense . . ."

He pulled open the gullwing doors of the cruiser and slipped inside. "I'm driving." For a second he gazed at the completely foreign array of controls and gauges.

Spartan turned to Lenina Huxley. "You're driving . . ."

* * *

It fell to Chief Earle to report to Mayor-Gov Raymond Cocteau on what was being done to locate and destroy Simon Phoenix. The chief was sweating, uneasy and self-conscious in the presence of the great leader, even if it was only via video phone. In contrast to his police chief the Mayor-Gov was so calm and serene it was scary.

"Enhance your calm, Chief," said Dr. Cocteau soothingly. "Please, share your disquietude."

"Mayor-Gov Cocteau," said Earle nervously, "it has been called to my attention that the branching possibility exists the escaped cryo-con, Mr. Simon Phoenix, may be on his way to the San Angeles Museum of Art and History.

"And what permutation leads you to this curious conclusion," Raymond Cocteau asked. "Do you expect him to be homesick for the old days?" The Mayor-Gov chuckled quietly, enjoying his own wit immensely.

Chief Earle shook his head. "No. No, sir. Are you not aware of the armory exhibit at that facility? We surmise that he will attempt to arm himself in the Hall of Violence."

Cocteau's face fell. "No, I hadn't considered that. Not for a moment . . ."

The Armory Room in the Hall of Violence was nothing if not comprehensive. The glass display cases lining the walls were crammed with weapons that told the whole history of man's ingenuity when it came to injuring, maiming, lacerating, mangling, dismembering, or slaughtering his fellow man.

The exhibit went back to the beginning of time,

displaying the crude weapons of the cavemen—
clubs, stone axes, and arrowheads. Then it moved
up through history, showing the horrified citizenry
of San Angeles how their ancestors had chopped
each other up in the Middle Ages, the Renaissance,
the Age of Enlightenment, and in the eighteenth,
nineteenth and twentieth centuries.

Simon Phoenix found any number of guns, but
nothing he really approved of. There were antiquated Colt pistols from the Old West, tommy guns
from the Roaring Twenties, and a big Civil War
cannon that sat in the middle of the room, flanked
by a pyramid of iron cannon balls.

"If this is the future," yelled Simon Phoenix,
"where are the fucking phaser guns?"

He kept moving down the line, through the First
World War and the Second World War, Korea, and
Vietnam. He skipped the eighties and the nineties
until he came to a weapon he didn't recognize at all.
A little card identified the mammoth weapon as the
Smith & Wesson Magnetic Accelerator Gun. AcMag
for short.

"I like it," said Phoenix with a grin. "Wrap it up.
I'll take it." He reared back and punched the glass
as hard as he could. His fist bounced off the glass.

"Ow!" He buried his bruised hand under his
armpit. "That smarts!"

He launched a kick at the glass and succeeded in
cracking it, but he still couldn't get to the weapon.

"Son of a bitch!" yelled Phoenix. He hated being
thwarted in anything.

A museum guard attracted by the commotion
came into the Hall of Violence, smiling pleasantly
at Phoenix.

"Mellow greetings," said the guard. "What seems to be your boggle?"

Phoenix gazed at the guard steadily. "My boggle . . . Ah yes, my boggle. My boggle is this: I am at the top of the food chain, and I would prefer to use tools, not bruise my hands and feet."

"Your hands and feet?" said the guard, mystified.

"That's right. I need a rock or a crowbar, but I can't seem to find any heavy object in this place. Tell me, what do *you* weigh?"

The guard was completely confused. "What do I weigh?"

"Let's find out," said Phoenix. He picked up the guard and shot-put the hapless man into the display. There was an impressive shower of broken glass. "You weigh enough," said Phoenix.

The shattering of the glass set off an alarm. It wasn't a strident siren or clanging bells, instead, in keeping with the mellow times, the alarm was nothing more than a serene voice chanting, "Please exit . . . Please exit . . . Please exit . . . Please exit . . ."

Simon Phoenix paid no attention to the alarm as he busily sorted through the weapons. He loaded a shotgun and tested it by blasting both barrels into another display case.

The alarm changed, the voice sounding a little more frantic. "Please exit rapidly . . . Please exit rapidly . . . Please exit rapidly . . . Please exit rapidly . . ."

The alarm was beginning to annoy him. Phoenix slapped two more cartridges into the shotgun and took aim at the alarm loudspeaker box.

He grabbed a bandolier of shotgun shells and slung them crisscross over his chest. The shotgun would come in handy, but what he really wanted was to use the cool gun of the future, the Magnetic Accelerator Gun. He grabbed the weapon and examined it. There weren't any bullets and no way to load them either. About the only thing Phoenix recognized was the trigger. He aimed and pulled— and nothing happened.

"Son of a bitch!" Then he spotted one of the CompuKiosk information booths on the far side of the room, and Phoenix strode over to it. He couldn't help himself—yet again, he pressed the ego boost button.

"That's a great-looking shirt," said the computer voice.

"Thanks," said Phoenix with a chuckle, "It's my favorite."

"You look great in that color," agreed the computer.

"Yeah. Okay. Enough. I hate ass kissers." He hit the information button.

Another voice came up. "Yes, museum patron. Have you a query?"

"Yeah," said Phoenix. "What's the matter with the Magnetic Accelerator Gun?"

Graphics flashed on the screen. Phoenix scanned them closely, as if committing the amazing flow of information to memory.

The computer droned out a series of facts. "The Magnetic Accelerator Gun, the last produced hand-held weapon of this millennium displaced the flow of neutrons through a nonlinear cycloid supercooled electromagnetic force."

"So . . . what?" demanded Phoenix. "It needs

new batteries? What size? Who sells batteries in the future? Is there a battery store I can go to?''

But before the machine-generated voice could respond, a real, human voice spoke to him. "Excuse me, museum patron, may I help you?''

Phoenix turned. Two museum security guards had come into the room and were standing between him and the exit. Phoenix didn't bother to banter with them. He leveled the shotgun and blasted. The force of the explosion cut down the two guards, blood and tissue splattering all over the place.

Sensing the blood and sudden violence, the museum security system changed the alarm tone again. "Run! Run! Run! Run!'' it said urgently. Steel doors dropped from the ceiling sealing the room.

The information computer had solved Simon Phoenix's problems with the AcMag weapon. "The Magnetic Accelerator *now* activated,'' it reported efficiently. "It will concurrently supercool and achieve fusion in two point six minutes.''

Phoenix glanced at the steel doors. "Yeah, well I was considering leaving quickly and patience is *not* one of my virtues.'' Phoenix shook his head. "Who am I kidding? I don't *have* any virtues.''

He chuckled at his own wit, then raced around the room, grabbing weapons and ammunition, gleefully scooping up firearms like a kid in a candy store.

One of the dummies was of a Vietnam-era GI, dressed in jungle fatigues and carrying a gunny sack. Phoenix grabbed the bag and stuffed his goodies into it.

"You don't mind if I borrow this, do ya, Rambo?''

* * *

Lenina Huxley's SAPD cruiser screeched to a halt in front of the Museum of Art and History, and the three police officers jumped out. People were streaming out of the museum building, and Huxley, Garcia, and Spartan had to fight against the flow of panicked people. A knot of spooked museum security guards were waiting for them at the main entrance.

"We have three murder-death-kills!" screeched one of them in disbelief. "Three!"

There was so much confusion that only Spartan noticed the makeshift periscope that popped out of the ground just ahead of them. The instant Spartan spotted it, the periscope zipped back down the hole.

"You see that?" Spartan asked.

"See what?" asked Garcia.

"Never mind," said Spartan. "I give up trying to figure this place out."

Garcia activated his Strategic Apprehension Computer. "Procedure?"

"Establish communication with the maniac intruder," advised the computer.

"Wrong," said Spartan. He grabbed the SAC from Alfredo Garcia and threw it to the ground, smashing it. "Hey, Luke Skywalker. Use the Force."

"You deliberately destroyed San Angeles police property," said Alfredo Garcia, his eyes bugging out.

"It slipped," said Spartan.

"You should be armed, John Spartan," said Huxley, handing him a stun baton.

He looked at without enthusiasm. "What the hell is this?"

"It's a glow rod," said Garcia. "It's what we use in violent situations."

"Does it work?" asked Spartan. He poked a nearby security guard who dropped like a dead weight. "Guess so."

"They have Phoenix trapped in section eight," said Huxley. She was anxious to get the operation underway.

"I wouldn't be so sure of that," said Spartan. "Phoenix has a way of getting around traps. Just make sure there's no one else in the building."

Huxley nodded. "Done." She turned to the security guards. "I want a visual. Now. Every corridor in the museum. I want full sensors routed to me. And I want it ninety seconds ago. Understand?"

The guards understood, and they jumped to carry out her orders. John Spartan looked at Lenina Huxley with something approaching respect. In the old days she probably would have made a pretty fair police officer.

"Okay," he said, moving into the building. "Let's go pay a call on Mr. Simon Phoenix." He swung his baton as he walked, wishing he had something a little more substantial than an electronic bat.

12

Spartan approached section eight, the Hall of Violence, and saw that the steel security doors were controlled by an emergency release, a red handle next to the entrance. He checked his baton and reached for the control, but before he could pull the lever, the steel doors exploded in a great gout of smoke and hot metal.

Spartan dove for the floor as a battered cannon ball bounced down the marble hall. Then he jumped to his feet and hurled himself through the twisted doors, rolled once and took cover behind one of the shattered exhibits.

Phoenix crouched behind the Civil War cannon, draped in guns and ammunition. He looked like a mad bandito. He surveyed his handiwork with pride. "What can I say? I'm a blast from the past!"

Spartan's voice rose out of the smoke. "You should have stayed there."

Phoenix squinted into the haze. "Who is that? That voice sounds familiar . . . Mom?" Simon unleashed a murderous round of machine gun fire from the Heckler and Koch 91 draped around his neck like a piece of black steel jewelry.

The murderous rate of fire shattered the remaining display cases. Glass and wood chips cascaded to the floor as the bullets chewed up the exhibits.

A rusty old Beretta tumbled out of one of the cases and landed right in front of John Spartan. He grabbed the ancient weapon, loaded it, and came up.

"Stop or I'll shoot! Phoenix! Do you hear me?" Spartan came up firing, getting off three shots before Phoenix began strafing the area with his machine gun again. Then he stopped firing as a jolt of recognition pulsed through him.

"Spartan! John Spartan!" Simon Phoenix almost sounded glad to see his old nemesis. "Well, finally somebody who knows how to party! Shit, they'll let anyone into this century. What are you doing here?"

"I pounded your ass once before, Phoenix," shouted Spartan. "I guess this is the sequel."

"Oh, really," Phoenix spat back. "When do the thirty innocent bystanders get greased? Right now, Simon says bleed!"

Phoenix started blazing away again, bullets ricocheting all around the shattered room. Then he stopped and picked up the AcMag and pulled the trigger. The high-tech weapon still refused to respond.

"Come on, you space age piece o' shit," Phoenix mumbled. He stuck the AcMag back in his belt. "Okay, well I guess we'll have to do this the old-fashioned way . . ."

He dumped a load of black powder into the canon. Then he lowered the HK 91 machine gun and strafed the room, just to make Spartan keep his head down. Then he tamped down the powder with the ram—and paused to strafe the room again.

Spartan was flat on the floor, taking cover as best he could. A few yards away, tantalizingly close, Spartan could see a twelve-gauge auto loader shotgun and a full box of shells. That powerful weapon would certainly come in handy. Gingerly, John Spartan started crawling toward it.

Phoenix was still busy loading the cannon. "So lemme get this straight," he shouted. "These guys defrosted you just to lasso my piddly ass?" Like punctuation, he let off a rip of machine-gun shells, emptying the magazine.

Calculating the odds, Spartan dove, rolling across the aisle, grabbing the gun, and then ducking for cover.

Phoenix had loaded one of the iron cannon balls into the muzzle of the ancient weapon, and he lit the fuse.

"I've been dreaming about killing you for forty years, Spartan."

"Keep dreaming," said John Spartan, jumping to his feet. He blasted away—there's a lot of fire power in a twelve-gauge used at close range. Phoenix answered with a pair of six-shooters, like an old-fashioned gun slinger.

The cannon was pointed straight at Spartan, too,

but a display case collapsed under the withering fire and hit the field piece, deflecting the muzzle until it was pointing straight down at the floor.

The cannon detonated, blowing straight into the floor, the whole support structure giving way, throwing both men through the floor and into the display on the level below. Smoke and fire erupted everywhere, and it took Spartan and Phoenix a few seconds to figure out what happened.

"Nice shooting," yelled Phoenix. "Really nice shooting, Spartan. You killed the building."

Then they saw where they were. Both men had fallen into the late twentieth-century display of the bad old Los Angeles. Spartan shook off the shock and realized that somewhere in the fall he had lost his gun.

No such luck with Phoenix. He still had his sack full of goodies, and he let fly with a skein of hot lead from a powerful MAC-10 machine pistol.

"Past is over, Spartan," yelled Phoenix. "No more bullets. It is time for something new and improved. Like me. Now die!" Phoenix yanked out the AcMag and fired. The weapon was completely silent, but the first object that intersected his aim simply exploded in a massive sheet of fire.

"Whoa!" Phoenix looked at his gun and cackled hysterically. "I *love* this thing!" He fired again, and a fire hydrant erupted, showering water down on the exhibit like a monsoon.

Water sprayed everywhere, and Phoenix stood in a puddle in a pothole in the middle of the dummy street. Spartan had an idea. He pulled out his stun baton, activated it, and jammed it into the stream of water.

"You forgot to say Simon says." The electricity gushed through the water, and suddenly Phoenix felt real pain as the power jolted through him. He used all his strength to pull himself out of the puddle.

"What a brave new world we live in now, Spartan," he screamed. "It's really a shame you have to leave." He raised the AcMag and fired. Everywhere he pointed his weapon, buildings and cars exploded in blinding balls of flame. Spartan was darting and weaving through the wreckage, a cloud of fire all around him. In the middle of the inferno he found the old Beretta again and managed to squeeze off a few shots, but they were like popgun shots compared to the murderous destruction of the AcMag.

Spartan knew he had to do something. He jumped out from cover and fired. But Phoenix was gone . . .

Given his exalted rank as Mayor-Gov, Dr. Raymond Cocteau was accorded the distinction of a long, large limousine, a vehicle three times bigger than any other car on the road. Cocteau and Associate Bob got to the museum just in time to see a column of thick dark smoke rising into the sky from the very center of the museum complex.

Associate Bob gulped nervously. "Sir, the Stress Breeder is inside being demobilized as we speak."

A bullet whizzed by his ear, barely missing the nervous man and he dropped face first into the dirt. Cocteau was a picture of calm. He turned and smiled at Phoenix, who was advancing on him, the AcMag stuffed into his belt. He had an old Luger in his hand. Phoenix liked the new weapon, but sometimes he wanted to do things the old-fashioned way.

"Damn," said Phoenix. "I guess being frozen has thrown off my aim. Don't worry, I'll kill you with my next shot."

Cocteau shook his head. "I don't think so."

Phoenix sneered. "Yeah? Watch me." He raised the weapon and aimed it squarely at Cocteau's head. But then something seemed to snap inside of him, and his smile turned to a grimace. Phoenix's gun hand quivered as he tried to pull the trigger— he wanted to kill, but he couldn't.

"Damn. *That's* never happened before."

Dr. Cocteau folded his arms. "Ah, no kiss kiss. No bang bang," he said. "And you were doing so well. Now don't you have a job to do? Don't you hear a thought repeating in that barbaric brain of yours—the name Friendly, Edgar Friendly. Don't you have someone to kill?"

Phoenix looked at the older man, surprised and puzzled at his words. His brow creased. "Yeah . . . Yeah, I do . . ."

Cocteau beamed. "Excellent! Then go and do your job. Civic responsibility is not to be avoided, you know."

"Right, man!" Phoenix took off, running for all he was worth, just as Spartan came racing out of the wreckage. Phoenix vaulted a wall and vanished.

Spartan took aim with the Beretta, but he had no shot. He lowered his gun. He turned to Cocteau and Associate Bob. "You don't know how lucky you are that maniac didn't whack you."

Cocteau smiled thinly. "No doubt 'whacking', whatever it is, would be most disagreeable. You scared him away, and I do not know how to thank you. You saved my life.''

Spartan looked in the direction Phoenix had gone, then back to Cocteau. Something strange was going on here—Phoenix killed anything that got in his way. And he didn't scare easily.

Garcia and Huxley, along with Chief Earle came racing up. Lenina was elated.

''Not bad for a seventy-four-year-old, John Spartan,'' she said. ''Now Simon Phoenix knows he has some competition! He's finally matched his meat and you really licked his ass.''

''Uh,'' said Spartan, ''that's met his match. And it's kicked. Kicked his ass.''

Cocteau took his police chief by the arm and walked him out of earshot of the rest. ''Who is this man?'' he asked coolly.

''It is Detective John Spartan,'' said Earle. ''He is temporarily reinstated to the San Angeles Police Department to pursue this madman, Simon Phoenix.'' Chief Earle was so distraught by all the mayhem that he was on the verge of tears. ''You instructed us to do everything in our power to capture this madman.''

Cocteau nodded. ''That is correct. Yes. Yes, I did. I do recall the exploits of John Spartan. Didn't they call him . . . I think it was . . .'' He glanced toward the burning building. ''Ah yes, he was the Demolition Man.''

Earle gulped and nodded. ''That's what he was called in the twentieth, Mayor-Gov. I am deeply sorry for the destruction he has caused.''

Cocteau put out a hand to calm the man. ''It's quite all right, Chief.'' He surveyed the damage.

"It's unexpected, creative in a strange sort of way. But quite all right. Be well, Chief Earle."

But Earle was still terrified. He just nodded to his superior and slunk away.

Cocteau turned to Spartan. "John Spartan, welcome. So what do you think of our fair society? It must be quite different from the noise and confusion of your sorry time."

"Great," said Spartan. "I come to the future, and Phoenix gets the ray gun and I get the rusty Beretta."

Cocteau raised his voice and opened his arms wide. "John Spartan, in honor of your arrival and for your protection of the sanctity of human life, namely my own, I wish for you to join me at dinner tonight." He smiled at Lenina Huxley. "In fact, both of you must join me. I insist. You must accompany me to Taco Bell this very evening."

Lenina Huxley looked overwhelmed at the invitation, flattered and pleased. But John Spartan looked puzzled.

"Taco Bell?"

"It is a restaurant," Lenina Huxley stage-whispered. "Our finest dining establishment."

"It is?" Huxley elbowed him sharply in the ribs. Spartan smiled at Cocteau. "Uh . . . dinner. That would be great. I'm looking forward to it."

Spartan was not happy.

Lenina Huxley and Alfredo Garcia, along with Chief Earle, had taken him back to the station, sat him down and tried to explain how things worked in the brave new twenty-first century—hence his unhappiness. He particularly did not go along with the idea of a single man engineering every facet of every person's life. For a rugged individualist like Spartan, one-man rule really stuck in his craw.

Furthermore, some of Cocteau's most prestigious accomplishments seemed to him to be the most loathsome.

"Let me get this straight," he said, scowling at a giant Cocteau on the video screen. His arms were spread wide as if bestowing his benediction on anyone who gazed at his image.

Spartan jerked a thumb at the picture of the leader. "Spacely Sprockets here, who is now in charge, the Mayor-Gov who wants to take me to Taco Bell—though Lord knows I wouldn't mind a burrito—is also one of the guys who invented the goddamn cryo-prison?"

The nearest morality box beeped. "John Spartan, you have been fined . . ." Spartan just snatched the piece of paper from the device and stuffed it in his breast pocket.

"Dr. Cocteau is the most important man in San Angeles," said Earle. "He practically created our whole way of life. Don't forget that, *savage!*"

"Well, he can have it," said Spartan. He chose his words carefully. "And rather than inserting barbed instruments up the rectums of those around you, why don't you sit on one yourself, Chief?"

Earle looked flustered and glanced at the morality box, as if expecting it to come to his defense. But it sat silent, but ever vigilant.

Lenina Huxley pulled up a huge schematic map of greater San Angeles, and Spartan studied it closely. "Phoenix could be anywhere, but not having a code in his hand could hurt him. Limit his options."

Lenina nodded. "That is correct. Money is outmoded. All transactions are through codes."

Spartan was thinking aloud now. "So Phoenix can't buy food or a place to crash for the night. Pointless for him to mug anybody." He was silent for a moment. "Unless he rips off someone's hand. Let's hope he hasn't figured out that one yet."

All of the cops looked nauseated at the image Spartan had conjured up.

"And with all the officers already patroling in a citywide crisis net, it should be just a matter of tick tocks before we have him," said Alfredo Garcia.

"And you know," put in Chief Earle, "we already have a backup plan. We can just wait for another code to go to red. When Phoenix performs another murder-death-kill, we'll know exactly where to pounce."

"Oh, great plan," said Spartan sardonically.

For once Chief Earle looked pleased. "Thank you."

Spartan turned his attention back to the map. "So where the fuck is he?"

The morality box burst into life. "John Spartan, you have been fined—"

"Yeah, yeah," said Spartan, grabbing the paper. "I heard that one already."

In actual fact Simon Phoenix was not that far away from the police station. He had managed to elude various units of the SAPD until he found a large, deep storm drain in an industrial part of the city.

He pried up the grate and slipped down into the gloom. "No front door, no welcome mat, what's with these people? How are you supposed to show up and kill someone?"

Simon Phoenix disappeared into the shadows, cackling with laughter. "I crack myself up!" he said, his voice echoing in the subterranean passage. "I really do."

Lenina Huxley prattled happily as she drove John Spartan to the Taco Bell and their dinner with Dr. Raymond Cocteau. She was a little embarrassed by the obviousness of her schoolgirl crush on her hero from the past. "I've been an enthusiast of your escapades for quite some time, John Spartan."

"Is that a fact?"

"I have, in fact, perused some actual newsreels of you in the Schwarzenegger Library. Like that time you drove your car through that—"

Spartan held up his hand. "Back up. The Schwarzenegger library?"

Huxley nodded. "Yes, the Schwarzenegger Presidential Library. Wasn't he an actor when you . . ."

Spartan's head reeled. "Stop . . . He was president?"

"Indeed," said Huxley. "Even though he was not born in this country, his popularity at the time caused the ratification of the sixty-first amendment which states—"

Spartan waved her off. "I don't want to know." He stared out the window, watching the people on the streets, staring at their faces, as if searching for someone.

"I keep looking around," he said softly. "Thinking about my daughter. She grew up in a place like this. I'm afraid she's going to think I'm some kind of disgusting primate from the past. As much as I want to see her, I almost don't want to know . . . I'm not going to fit into the picture very well. She'll probably hate me . . ."

Lenina Huxley reached for the car computer terminal. She was grinning slyly, as if thrilled by her little bit of mischief. "It would be a minor misuse of police powers, but I could do another search for you."

Spartan reached over to stop her, touching her

hand. But then he remembered that touching was frowned upon in the new society. However, Lenina didn't seem to mind the contact. He shook his head.

"It's no trouble," she said.

Spartan changed the subject. "So what's with this Cocteau guy? He thanks me for saving his life—which I'm not sure I did—and my reward is dinner and dancing at *Taco Bell*. I mean, hey, I like Mexican food but come on . . ."

Lenina Huxley looked perplexed. "Your tone is quasi facetious. You do not realize Taco Bell was the only restaurant to survive the Franchise Wars?

"So?" said Spartan.

"So, now all restaurants are Taco Bell!"

"Great," said Spartan.

A few moments later they pulled up in front of the Taco Bell—except it was like no Taco Bell Spartan had ever seen before. First of all, it was huge and luxurious. A group of parking valets stood in front of the building, and one of them rushed over to relieve Lenina of her vehicle.

She led the way inside. The interior of the restaurant was dark and cool, ultrahip and elegant in that casually urbane way of the best California restaurants.

The place was spare and understated and the patrons cool and beautiful. As were the counter help. To John Spartan the girls behind the cash registers looked like haughty high-fashion models, the kind of women who were always unapproachable in the old world.

But the counter girl broke out of the ultracool character of the place and suddenly smiled a typical fast-food happy face. "Welcome!" she squeaked. "May I help you?"

Spartan was taken aback by this sudden reverse. "Uh, I'll take a burrito supreme," he said. "And a shake."

"Copy that," said Lenina.

"Will that be for here or to go?"

"Ah," said Spartan attempting to be charming. "The eternal question . . . Here."

The counter girl did a perky fast-food spin to the serving hatch and whipped back with an ornate silver tray carrying an elaborate china set.

"Two burrito supremes. Two shakes," she said with a smile. "Be well."

Spartan looked down at the minuscule cylinder of pressed kelp topped with a dab of salsa and a sprinkle of sesame bits. "Yum," he said. "It's a good thing I'm hungry."

Spartan and Lenina carried their trays into the restaurant, escorted by a maître d' wearing a stiff black dinner jacket. He guided them to a secluded section of the restaurant in front of one of the windows, where Cocteau and Associate Bob were waiting for their dinner guests.

Cocteau stood and addressed the restaurant. "Gentlemen, allow me to present my savior, Detective John Spartan." He raised his shake and sipped.

"Greetings and salutations, I am Associate Bob," the man said with an ingratiating smile. "We have met before, but ever so briefly when I was groveling in fear at the time. You have had quite the exciting first day in our fair city. Imagine, a real criminal loose in San Angeles!"

Spartan sat down. "Imagine that." He picked up

the burrito and could tell just by looking at it that it needed something to perk it up. "Could someone pass me the salt?"

Lenina Huxley whispered. "Salt is not good for you. Hence it is—"

Spartan glared at her, and she shut up quickly. He poked at his food, but he seemed to have lost his appetite.

"So, John Spartan," Cocteau said, "tell me, what do you think of San Angeles, A.D. 2032."

Spartan shrugged. He didn't want to be rude. "I guess, considering the way things were going when I went in—I thought the future would be a rotting cesspool."

"You should consider visiting New York after this," said Associate Bob.

Spartan brightened. "You mean nothing has changed?"

Associate Bob roared with laughter, as if Spartan had gotten off a particularly witty bon mot. Spartan just stared at him hard and turned back to his food. It was obvious to Cocteau if not to Associate Bob that Spartan was less than thrilled with the fine fare the future had to offer.

"Look at you, John Spartan," Cocteau said with a smile. "I can see you're pouting for the old cheeseburger—the flesh of dead animals covered with cholesterol-laden butterfat. You miss the bad old days."

Spartan put down the burrito and rested his elbows on the table. "Put it this way, Dr. Cocteau, I like vegetables. I even got reckless and ate yogurt a couple of times. The point is I got to choose when and how I wanted it."

Cocteau nodded. "I understand," he said. "The democratic process isn't dead—it's only been modified. Of course, you weren't here for the forth and fifth riots."

Spartan looked grave. He had no idea there had been more riots after he had been cryo-imprisoned.

Cocteau's voice was harsh. "Civilization tried to destroy itself. The city degenerated into a total fear zone. The citizenry cocooned in their homes, afraid to come out. People just wanted the madness to be over. So when I saw the opportunity to make things right, I acted promptly. If I had not, the radiance of San Angeles would not be here, just the rotting cesspool of suffering and hate you envisioned."

Cocteau stared hard at Spartan, an arrogant sense of knowing in his steely eyes. "Tell me John Spartan, which would you prefer?"

Spartan met the Mayor-Gov's stare. "Maybe you can book me a flight to the East Coast when the sermon is over."

Lenina Huxley's mouth dropped open. She couldn't imagine that anyone could talk to the Mayor-Gov like that. Cocteau's face darkened. He was not used to people contradicting him. He preferred subjects like Associate Bob—supine and slavishly grateful.

"For your crimes, John Spartan, you would have surely rotted and died in jail by now. Even *you* have to appreciate the persuasively tranquil humanity of the cryo-prison system."

It was Spartan's turn to scowl. He did not need to be reminded of his long, horrible sentence in that frozen hell. "I don't want to spoil your dinner, pal, but my cryo sentence wasn't a sweet lullaby."

He lowered his voice, as if the pain of recalling it was physical as well as mental. "I had feelings—I had thoughts. A thirty-six-year nightmare about all those people trapped in a burning building."

Cocteau looked at him sharply. "You were awake? I don't think so, my friend."

Spartan face twisted in anger. "I *do* think so. I had thoughts, I had feelings—about my wife beating her fists against a block of ice that used to be her husband. Then you were nice enough to wake me up and let me know everything that meant something in my life is gone. It would have been more humane to stake me down and leave me to the fucking crows."

There was no morality box at Dr. Cocteau's table.

Huxley was puzzled. "I thought during rehabilitation prisoners were not conscious. A person would go insane."

"The side effects of the cryo-process are unavoidable," said Cocteau in his own defense. "You were found guilty of criminal charges and owed—and still owe—a debt to society. I'm sorry, but there's nothing I can do . . ."

But Spartan was not paying attention. He was staring out the window. First there had been two Scraps lolling outside the Taco Bell. Then three . . . then four. Then one drove up on a rickety old motorcycle, a machine patched together with the parts of a dozen older bikes. The scraps were loitering and looking around shiftily. To Spartan's practiced eye, they were up to no good.

A food van rumbled down the street toward the restaurant.

Spartan stood up. "There's one thing you can do for me," he said.

"What?" asked Huxley.

"Call for backup. I'll be across the street—"

"But John Spartan, why? How? What are you going to do?"

Spartan was strolling toward the door. "There are bad guys about to do bad things . . . It's just one of those cop hunches."

14

Spartan strode out of the front door of the Taco Bell, walking in such a way that he could never be mistaken for another satisfied Taco Bell patron. He radiated attitude—and the Scraps could tell with a single glance that Spartan was trouble. The thin, skaggy-looking guy mounted on the equally ragtag motorcycle gunned the bike a couple of times and then popped it in gear, roaring toward him.

Quickly, Spartan grabbed the VALET PARKING sign, uprooting the pole from the ground and holding it at the ready.

The motorcycle may have been old and rusty, but the Scrap managed to coax all of the power possible out of the screaming engine. He was roaring straight at Spartan, ready to run him over. Spartan stood his ground.

It seemed as if the front wheel of the bike was on him when Spartan swung into action, the long pole cutting a wide swath in the air, smacking into the Scrap's chest, knocking him from the saddle.

The motorcycle skidded by Spartan, hit the curb, somersaulted, and exploded in a ball of flame. Spartan didn't flinch, but the clients of the Taco Bell dove for cover as the motorcycle detonated.

The Scraps rushed at Spartan, but each of them went down under a furious fusillade of blows, the weedy youths being mowed down like green wheat. They toppled so readily and made such basic mistakes in the art of attack and defense that Spartan had to assume they were new to the business of being tough guys.

Suddenly, though, the Scraps upped the ante. A manhole cover blew out of the roadbed like a bomb and out jumped a half dozen more fighters, and these looked a little more determined. They carried bicycle chains and homemade nunchucks, and a couple of them looked as if they might have a clue as to how to use them.

"Great," muttered Spartan. "They brought the whole team." He knocked two of his attackers senseless, felling them with rib-crunching body blows. "Now if we can just get them to stay and play."

Spartan dodged one of the Scraps wielding an old aluminum baseball bat, cracked him on the back of the head, and then turned for the next onslaught.

But the Scraps had lost interest in him. They had fallen on the food van and were frantically tearing at the food pods. Some were packing food into canvas sacks, others were stuffing it right into their mouths, wolfing down the makings of a thousand burritos, as if they hadn't eaten in a month.

"Protein!" shouted one of them. "I've found protein!"

This brought Spartan up short.

"Protein?" That didn't strike him as the sort of thing that a hardened criminal would be particularly interested in. "What's going on?"

By way of an answer, one last valiant Scrap landed a nunchuck blow on Spartan's brawny shoulder. The young man stepped back both appalled and proud of what he had done.

Spartan stared at the astonished Scrap, watching as he summoned up his courage and came in for another attack. He hit Spartan again, but the blow evinced no reaction at all. He swung his nunchuck again, putting all of his force behind the attack, but this time Spartan's rock-hard fist shot out and stopped the blow dead in midair. He swung the hapless Scrap by the end of his chain and threw him like a bowling ball into the crowd of Scraps gathered around the food van. They tumbled like ninepins.

"You're all under arrest," said Spartan.

From the middle of the tangle of arms and legs Edgar Friendly struggled to his feet. He looked at Spartan, a sneer on his face. He didn't know who this guy was, but he did know that the big cop was working the wrong side of the law.

"What a fucking hero!" he snarled. He helped one of his fellow Scraps to his feet and then shouldered a food pod. "Come on!" he ordered. "We're outta here!"

The Scraps stumbled to their feet, each tottering under the burden of the food. Spartan stared hard, trying to figure out just what the hell was going on. He took a step toward the frantic throng, and the Scrap nearest him dropped to his knees, cowering in fear, cans of food tumbling from his tattered jacket.

"Please . . . don't . . . Please don't hurt me," the young man pleaded. The Scrap was plainly in fear for his life, and something in Spartan made him stop. He just watched as the ragtag band darted back down the into the sewers from whence they came.

Suddenly, Lenina Huxley was at his side. "Such reckless abandonment!" she said, her eyes glowing in admiration. "Looks like there's a new shepherd in town."

"Sheriff," said Spartan, watching the last of the Scraps escape. "That's sheriff."

"You were magnificent, John Spartan!" she cried.

"Who were those guys?"

"We call them Scraps," said Cocteau. He was striding toward Spartan, and it was plain that he was not happy. Associate Bob scuttled along at his side. "They are voluntary outcasts. They cower beneath us in sewers, in abandoned tunnels—creatures of the darkness."

Associate Bob took his cue from his boss. "They're nothing but thugs and hooligans," he said vehemently. "A society of thieves."

"Thieves?" said Spartan. "I thought there weren't any thieves here in paradise."

"They are the last criminal element in the entire megacity," said Associate Bob. "Plans are in progress to purge this peril once and for all."

Cocteau nodded appreciatively. His underling had quoted perfectly from the collected speeches of Mayor-Gov Dr. Raymond Cocteau.

"Peril? They didn't seem so perilous to me," said Spartan. "They just seemed hungry."

Lenina was still high from watching her hero in action. "That's only because you are used to much greater dangers, John Spartan. You were even better live than on laser disc. Oh, and the joy-joy way you paused to make glib witticisms before doing battle with the strangely weaponed Scrap. It was so . . . so . . ."

Spartan shook his head. "Hey," he said, angrily. "This isn't the wild west. The wild west wasn't even the wild west. Hurting people is not my idea of a good time."

"It isn't?" asked Lenina. All of her research had caused her to believe that John Spartan was a violence professional who genuinely enjoyed his work. How could she have been so wrong about him?

"Well . . ." admitted John Spartan. "Sometimes it is. It all depends on who it is. Simon Phoenix is fair game. But when it's a bunch of guys who are hungry . . . That's wrong. Dead wrong." He shook his head sadly. "You know, I think I liked it better when we were all supposed to fry in a nuclear holocaust. It was . . . fairer."

Spartan shot an angry glance at Cocteau, then walked away. Lenina Huxley gasped and swallowed. She could not believe that anyone would dare to talk to the Mayor-Gov in such a disrespectful manner. She looked to Dr. Cocteau who was glowering at Spartan as he strode away.

Lenina chased after him, determined to stop him from making another terrible mistake.

It took her a while to calm Spartan enough to coax him into her car. She drove him through the darkened city, glancing worriedly at him as he sat in the passenger seat, staring straight ahead.

Finally, he took a deep breath and did his best to quell his anger.

"Look," he said softly. "I'm sorry I lost my temper, back there—"

Lenina shook off his apology. "No need to make a dehurtful retraction. I've assimilated too much contraband, and I made a mistake about you."

"You did?"

Lenina nodded. "I fleshed you as some 'blow up the bad guys with a happy grin he man' type, but I realize now that you're the 'moody troubled past gunslinger who only draws when he must' type."

Spartan sighed heavily, shaking his head wearily. She just didn't get it. "Huxley. Stop. I'm not any of those things. I just did my job and . . ." he shrugged. "Things got demolished. It just happened that way."

Lenina just stared at the enigma seated next to her. Then she picked up a small flat box and handed it to him.

"Hey, here's a subject change. Here's what you asked for." She passed it to him. "Why do you need this?"

Spartan pocketed it. "Thanks. It's just a hunch."

"You don't want to tell me about it?"

Spartan shook his head. "Too soon."

Lenina guided the car on to the off ramp of the

freeway, and the car whirred up to the forecourt of a huge, gleaming silver geometric building.

Spartan gazed up at the huge tower. It seemed to reach into the clouds. "This is where you live?"

"You live here, too," said Lenina with a smile. "I have procured you a domicile just down the corridor from my own."

The elevator shot them up to the high floors, as if it had been fired from a field piece, then Lenina led him down a long corridor to her apartment.

"Everything is voice coded," she explained, walking into the dark apartment. "So if you need something . . . just ask. Lights!"

The lights came up immediately. In a day filled with surprises, it may have been Lenina's apartment that surprised him most. There was little of 2032 here—she had tried to re-create the ambiance of a 1990s apartment. However, like someone who has learned everything from books without experiencing the real thing, she had just missed getting it right.

There was a shag rug on the floor, and all the furniture was upholstered in a riot of crushed red velour. Posters of monster trucks covered the walls, and odd nickknacks were scattered on the tables and bookshelves. If Huxley had hoped to decorate her apartment like that of a 1990s sophisticate, she was way off; the effect was more preteen meets smalltime drug dealer.

Of course Spartan was far too polite to say anything that might hurt her feelings.

"What do you think?" she asked proudly. "I clicked off a lot of credits to create the perfect twentieth-century apartment. Nice, huh?"

"It's very . . ." He wasn't sure just what, but it certainly was *very*. He nodded, hoping he was implying approval.

"Isn't it?" she said with a smile.

"Absolutely!"

She seemed to glow with pleasure. Then she looked down at the floor. "John Spartan," she said. "There is, of course, a well-known and documented connection between sex and violence."

"There is?"

Lenina shrugged. "Well . . . not so much a causal effect, but a state of general neurological arousal."

Spartan stared, wondering just what the hell she was getting at now.

"After observing your behavior at the Taco Bell and by analyzing my resultant condition, I was wondering if you would like to have sex."

She was looking right at him now, a slightly lascivious cast to her lips.

There would never be an end to the weirdness of this day, he thought. "Sex?"

Lenina Huxley nodded. "That's right."

"With you?"

Lenina nodded. "Affirmative."

"Now?"

Lenina laughed. "Of course! Why should we delay? Seize the moment!"

This was one piece of the twenty-first century that Spartan liked. No more fussing around with dinners and flowers—get straight to the point. It had been a long time since John Spartan had had sex, and he could definitely use some action right now. But his upbringing and basic instincts told him not to appear all that eager.

"Ahhh . . . ahhh . . . mmmmm . . . yeah," he said with a shy grin. "I'd love to have sex."

"Great!" said Huxley perkily. She turned quickly and pulled two strange silver-toned helmets and a fluffy white towel from a cabinet in a corner of the living room. Rapidly, she slipped the helmet over Spartan's head and buckled it on tight. She flicked a switch on the side of the helmet and the device hummed quietly and a red light blinked for a few moments before shifting to green.

Lenina Huxley settled on the sofa, slipped into her helmet, and turned it on. She placed the towel between them. A slightly dreamy look crossed her pretty face.

"Now you have to relax," she said softly. "We'll start in a few seconds."

"Start what?"

"Having sex, of course. Just wait."

Suddenly, the helmet's power kicked in, and Lenina appeared before Spartan's eyes, floating a few inches off the ground. Her image was wearing a diaphanous gown, the filmy material blowing gently around her slim body.

She wafted toward Spartan, slowly peeling off pieces of her dress, which seemed to dissolve into thin air, vanishing in a matter of seconds. She unwound the upper part of her gown, revealing her firm, full breasts . . .

Spartan stared in openmouthed amazement—and enjoyment—until he realized what was going on. He pulled off his helmet and threw it aside, confusion and anxiety on his face.

The erotic, provocative image vanished, and he

saw that Lenina was still sitting on the couch, fully clothed.

"What's wrong?" she asked. "You broke contact."

"Contact?" said Spartan. "I haven't even touched you yet!"

Lenina removed her helmet. Now it was her turn to look confused and hurt. "Touch?"

Spartan was completely flummoxed now. "Right."

"But I thought you wanted to make love."

"Is that what you call *this*?" Spartan waved the sensory helmet in her face.

Lenina was flustered now. She jumped to her feet, red in the face with anger and rejection. "Vir sex has been proven to produce higher orders of alpha waves during digitized transference of sexual energies!"

"Well, that's just great," said Spartan, laughing. "But what do you say we just do it the old-fashioned way?"

She stared at him, backing away in shock and disgust. Lenina couldn't believe he had even suggested such a thing.

"Ugh!" she said, sickened at the very idea. "Are you suggesting . . ." She could hardly bring herself to say the words. "*Fluid transfer*?" she said with a shudder.

Spartan grinned. "I mean boning, doing the wild mambo, you know"—he pumped his hips like a bad Elvis impersonator—"the hunka chunka."

"*That is no longer done!*" Lenina gasped. "It is out of the question!"

Spartan looked at her as if she had finally, ultimately, lost her mind. "No longer done? How is that possible?"

"Exchange bodily fluids? Do you know what that leads to?"

Spartan grinned. "Yeah. Sure. It leads to having kids, smoking, a desire to raid the fridge . . ."

Lenina refused to be amused. "The rampant exchange of bodily fluids was one of the major reasons for the downfall of your society." She took a deep breath, trying to calm herself. "After AIDS there was NRS. After NRS there was UBT."

"There was?" said Spartan, nonplussed. "Hey. I've been asleep for thirty years. I'm clean."

Lenina shook her head vigorously. "That doesn't matter. One of the first things Dr. Cocteau was able to do was outlaw and behaviorally engineer all fluid transfer out of socially acceptable behavior. Not even mouth transfer is condoned."

Now Spartan was really taken aback. "There's no kissing anymore? I was a good kisser. Great, just great. Dr. Cocteau finds the one peaceful thing I'm good at—and he outlaws it. That guy is no fun."

Lenina was still repulsed at the idea of what he had wanted to do to her. "Yuk," she said.

"What about kids?" asked Spartan. "Where do all the little Leninas and Alfredos come from?"

"You mean procreation?" said Lenina. "We go to the lab. Fluids are purified, screened, and transferred by authorized medical personnel only. It's the only legal way."

Spartan grinned and reached for her.

"What are you doing?" she said, pulling away.

"Breaking the law."

Huxley was outraged and she jumped to her feet.

"You are a savage creature! John Spartan, I wish you to leave my domicile now!"

She pointed toward the door and stamped her foot. "Out!"

"But . . . I was only trying to—"

"I don't care! Please leave immediately! Go to domicile 2261-C!"

Spartan just shook his head and walked out the door. "Some things just never change," he said.

The door slammed behind him.

Spartan hunted around the vast building for some time before he found his apartment. Because there was no crime in the future, there were no locks on the door of his apartment. He groped his way into the living room and stood in the dark.

"Ahh . . . Lights!" he said, feeling really stupid to be talking to no one. He would have felt better if there had been a light switch—even a clapper—because what so hard about replacing a light switch. Turning on lights had never been a hassle in the past. This was just change for change's sake.

Spartan's new home had all the charm of the interior of an abandoned refrigerator. It was the same size and shape as Lenina Huxley's, but even her misguided attempts at interior decorating had made the place warm. The huge vid screen dominated the room, the slate gray of the monitor as blank as a blind eye.

This apartment was sterile, devoid of any human touches—except for the cryo-package of his personal effects delivered from the prison and a ball of bright red yarn and a pair long knitting needles.

Spartan's hands started to quiver when he got near the ball of wool, as if he was drawn to the stuff.

He stared at his own hands, amazed at this involuntary reaction. He tore himself away from the yarn and threw himself into a spectacularly, uncomfortably futuristic chair and gazed into space.

A moment later, when Spartan looked down, he found the needles in his hands and he was unconsciously knitting with consummate skill. His fingers froze as he gaped in perplexed surprise. *He didn't know how to knit!*

Suddenly, the vid screen burst into life and a completely naked woman appeared on the screen. She was busily flossing her teeth and staring at her own image in the mirror.

"Hi, Martin," she said. "I was thinking . . ." She glanced in her mirror and saw Spartan staring at her in astonishment. "Oh, my God! I'm sorry, wrong number!" The woman reached for a switch off screen and suddenly her image vanished.

Up to that moment Spartan had not realized that the screen was a telephone. He thought a moment, then called out to the telescreen. "Uh, telephone directory . . . please."

Instantly, the machine responded. "Videophone directory accessed." The voice was male and cold, all business and computerized efficiency.

Spartan almost backed out, unnerved by the machine, but finally he summoned up his courage and spoke. "Do you have a number for Katie . . ." he began, then corrected himself. "Uh, I guess that's Katherine now. Last name, Spartan. Or maybe under her mom's name . . . Warren, or . . ." Then the terrible thought hit him. "Her mom may have remarried. But she's passed away now . . ." Suddenly, Spartan realized that he was rambling, pouring out his heart to a machine. He stopped talking, flustered that he had embarrassed himself in front of a machine.

The videoscreen had searched its vast brain and responded quickly. "There is no reference for Katie Spartan. There is no reference for Katherine Spartan. No current reference for Katherine Warren."

"No current reference?" Spartan queried. "Was there one?"

"Listed offspring under Madeline Warren through 2010. Listed different number domicile until 2028."

Spartan leaned forward in the uncomfortable chair. "What happened then?"

"No reference," said the computer. It seemed to Spartan that the machine had suddenly gone all tight-lipped, like a poker player guarding his cards.

"Did she die?" Spartan asked, dreading the answer.

"No death certificate issued. No reference."

"Good thing she didn't die without permission," said Spartan acidly. "Did she move?"

"No relocation license granted," replied the computer. "No reference."

Spartan was getting annoyed at this machine that was so sparing with the details of his daughter's life. "Reason for no reference?"

But the vid screen brain had gone as far as it intended. "What number do you wish to call?"

"Why don't you give Elvis a call?" said Spartan sourly.

The telescreen was programmed not to accept abusive, threatening, or crank calls.

"Be well," it said and hung up on him.

"I'll bet you don't mean that," said Spartan.

He stood and paced the room for a moment, wondering what to do next. More than anything, he wanted to find his daughter, but that would have to wait until he knew the lay of the land a little better.

That left the mystery—what had happened to Simon Phoenix. That he could do something about.

He remembered the small box Lenina Huxley had given him. He pulled it out of his pocket and opened it. Inside was a stack of wafer-thin laser minidiscs retrieved from the security cameras at the San Angeles Museum of Art and History.

Spartan slid the first one into the tray of the laserdisc reader in the base of the vid screen. It was a crystal clear picture of the explosion of the Hall of Violence, taken at the moment that smoke and debris went shooting through the roof. It was a high-quality picture—but it told him nothing.

The next slide was more revealing. This time surveillance had picked up a shot of Dr. Cocteau and Associate Bob walking through the courtyard of the museum.

Spartan loaded the third disc into the machine. This was a blurred image, catching Associate Bob in a dead fall, halfway to the slate floor. Cocteau was flinching, and a smudge of smoke blurred the corner of the picture. This must have been a stop-action shot of the single bullet Simon Phoenix had fired at the two men.

The final image was the most arresting. It showed Cocteau and Simon Phoenix having their face-to-face meeting. Spartan studied the picture closely. The two men appeared to be talking, conferring almost. There was not a hint of menace in Phoenix's eyes, and neither Cocteau nor Associate Bob appeared to fear for their lives. Spartan stared and wondered just what the spookily serene Mayor-Gov and the homicidal maniac could possibly be talking about.

John Spartan was so lost in thought he didn't even notice that unconsciously he had reached for the wool and was busily knitting, the clicking of the needles the only sound in the room.

15

For Mayor-Gov Dr. Raymond Cocteau it had been a very bad night—the worst he could remember for a very long time. First, Simon Phoenix had literally burst onto the scene, and he was proving even more difficult than his awesome reputation suggested. The Mayor-Gov had hoped that Phoenix would have been better programmed while he slept.

Then, to make matters worse, that jackass, Chief Earle, had gone and cryo-paroled the only man in history to subdue Simon Phoenix, John Spartan. For the time being, it seemed that Spartan could be controlled—despite his temper and temperament, John Spartan was a police officer; he understood authority, and Cocteau had a feeling that Spartan could be held in check—for a little while, anyway.

Furthermore, Dr. Cocteau knew for a fact that

Spartan did not have all the skills to operate at peak efficiency in this new world. That, more than anything, would slow down this unpredictable police officer.

But the worst thing that had happened, the most humiliating event of all, was the sudden appearance of Edgar Friendly and his ragtag band of followers— right before Cocteau's eyes. And Spartan had refused to do anything about it. In fact, he had demonstrated a distinct sympathy for the Scraps. *That* was not a promising development, and the Mayor-Gov would have to take steps to make sure that Spartan's empathy did not increase.

Therefore, it was not surprising that Cocteau was not in the best of moods when he finally got back to his office in the government center. Associate Bob trotted dutifully at his master's heels, well aware of the Mayor-Gov's black humor and wondering what he could do to alleviate it.

Cocteau stepped into his darkened office. "Lights," he ordered.

But the computer did not respond, and the room remained wreathed in sepulchral darkness.

"I said *lights*!"

From the dark came a cackling laugh. "Nahh," said Simon Phoenix. "I changed that. Just for the hell of it. Now you gotta say illuminate."

The lights clicked on, and Dr. Cocteau and Associate Bob were shocked and chagrined to see the master maniac sitting behind the Mayor-Gov's desk, his dirty boots squarely up on the pristine blotter.

Phoenix laughed again. "Illuminate!"

Sylvester Stallone as John Spartan.

Wesley Snipes as Simon Phoenix.

Simon Phoenix's headquarters explode in a fiery blaze . . .

. . . and police officer John Spartan is held responsible for the loss of innocent lives.

Spartan is taken to meet his fate in the Cryo Prison.

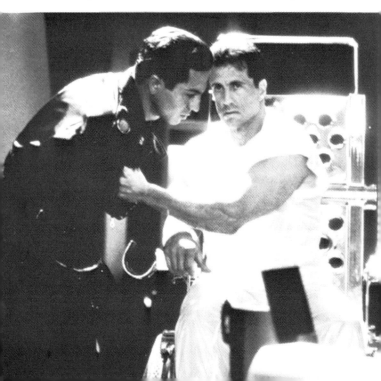

Awakened from his cryo chamber in 2032, Phoenix immediately resumes his life of crime and violence.

The authorities must release Spartan, the only man capable of stopping Phoenix's new reign of terror.

The future city of San Angeles is controlled by numerous department figureheads who communicate only through television screens.

Spartan ultimately must confront Dr. Raymond Cocteau
(Nigel Hawthorne), the Mayor/Governor of San Angeles in
the year 2032 and the father of Behavioral Engineering.

The lights turned off, and in the darkness Cocteau could be heard groaning in exasperation.

"Isn't that nicer?" asked Phoenix, teasing the two men. "Go ahead, Doc, you try it."

"Illuminate," said Cocteau acidly. The lights blinked on. "Very well, Phoenix. Let's stop playing."

"Raymond, buddy," said Phoenix, his voice full of mock sincerity. "That's why I'm here. We have a lot to talk about, right?"

"How did you get in?" Cocteau asked.

Phoenix shrugged and laughed again. "I wish I knew. Pass codes, routes to secret underground kingdoms. It's all in the computer." Phoenix shook his head in wonderment. "Check this out—I punch in one code and the machine goes, 'complete access to the industrial data grid interface.'" He flashed the two men a big grin.

"And I don't even know what that means," he said. "Not bad, huh? Not bad for a man who didn't know how to use a fucking toaster." Needless to say, Mayor-Gov Raymond Cocteau's private office was not equipped with a morality box.

"Now you do," said Cocteau.

"That's right. I've been meaning to ask you about it. But I want you to know that I like this. I like it. I like it a lot. Makes life so much easier."

Cocteau attempted to keep his calm demeanor, but Phoenix was annoying him mightily. "Your skills were given to you for a reason. And not for your personal amusement. Try to remember that."

"I never forget it, Ray, baby."

"Your job is to kill this disharmonious and disruptive young man, Edgar Friendly."

"Check," said Simon Phoenix.

"And once you have done that, you are to put a stop to a revolution before it precipitates. Which is what you were cryo-rehabbed to do."

Phoenix shrugged. "Yeah? Maybe I got a memory lapse, but I don't remember putting an application in for this particular gig. What did I do to get it?"

Cocteau was matter-of-fact. "It is a job that simply cannot be done by anyone else in San Angeles. No one is equipped, psychologically, to perform it. Barbaric skills such as yours are no longer needed in this society."

Phoenix took his feet off the desk and leaned forward to confront the two men. "Ahh," he said, "I would have to say you're wrong there, bud. Clearly, skills such as mine are very valuable these days. I think you've misjudged the situation." He sounded like a regional manager of some big corporation, dressing down a field salesman.

"Let's discuss, Raymond. Let's explore our options here. Find out what's really going on."

Cocteau shook his head. "All you need to do is kill Friendly and not allow his band of miscreants to wreak havoc anymore—surface-harassing havoc."

The Mayor-Gov was still fuming over the sudden appearance of the Scraps at the Taco Bell.

"Your ineptitude allowed it to grow worse tonight. Not fifty yards from where I was standing Edgar Friendly and his rabble attacked a food van. *You* were supposed to prevent this. And you didn't."

Phoenix stared hard at the man, his eyes narrowing. Associate Bob was getting a little nervous—

was there a chance that this maniac could explode and harm them both.

"Ineptitude?" Phoenix said "Now I would say that's a bit of a provocative word, Raymond, wouldn't you?"

"No," snapped Cocteau, "I wouldn't."

"You wouldn't?" said Simon Phoenix. "Have you ever been down to the Wasteland, Ray? Has *anyone* you know been down there? Do you really know anything about what goes on down there? No?"

Raymond Cocteau and Associate Bob were silent. Phoenix was pleased. Their silence told him all he needed to know. In fact, *they* didn't know about conditions in the subterranean city inhabited by the Scraps. That gave Simon Phoenix ample opportunity to lie through his teeth—and to scare the good doctor and his lapdog half to death.

"Well lemme tell you guys . . . it's bad down there—really bad. It's a wonder I got out of there alive. It's gonna be a big problem. Bigger than just one man can handle—even one with my skills."

"What do you suggest," said Cocteau, tight-lipped.

Phoenix looked as if he was genuinely sorry to have to suggest this, but . . .

"I'm gonna need five or six more guys. Five or six, easy. And I hope you got a list. 'Cause, see, I don't wanna defrost no serial killers or mad-dog types."

Cocteau smiled and folded his arms. He was beginning to understand what was going on. "So you're gonna be the only mad-dog type?"

But Phoenix didn't care if Cocteau had twigged to his plans. "Exactemundo, Doc."

"Fine. If that is what's required to resolve this situation," he said, his words clipped. Cocteau turned to Associate Bob. "Take care of it."

Associate Bob nodded and hurried to do his master's bidding. Cocteau turned back to Phoenix. "I'm telling you this—just get it over with. You're beginning to be more trouble than you're worth."

"Aww, don't say that," said Phoenix with a chuckle. "You'll hurt my feelings."

"Perish the thought. I would hate to do that."

"Good," said Phoenix. He thought for a moment. "By the way, what *am* I worth. What do I get out of all of this?"

Cocteau looked grim. He knew it was bound to come down to this eventually. "What do you want?"

"Well . . ." said Phoenix coyly. "I like to run things. Beyond murder and mayhem, I think I have some really first-rate managerial skills."

Cocteau tried to humor this frightening, threatening visitor from the past. "Perhaps you could become head of one of the city functions. A supervisor."

"You mean like garbage, fireman, light and power?" Phoenix shook his head. "Nah . . . I was thinking more in terms of real estate management."

"What are you talking about? Real estate?"

Phoenix stretched luxuriantly in the huge desk chair. "I'm talking about Malibu, Santa Monica . . . Maybe all the coastal cities."

Cocteau had no alternative but to agree to meet

Phoenix's demands—for the time being, at least. "I'll take it under advisement, Phoenix."

"We can exchange memos," said Phoenix.

Cocteau had had enough. "Before we get into the subject of reward, I would like to remind you that you have a job to do first. Once you have neutralized all the threats to San Angeles—and I mean *all*, Phoenix—we will discuss a suitable remuneration. Just do your job first. Now you may leave."

But Simon Phoenix wasn't quite ready to bring the discussion to a close.

"What the hell is Spartan doing here, Raymond?" Phoenix looked really annoyed. "Who invited him to our party? I don't like that at all."

Cocteau had hoped this question wouldn't come up. Spartan wasn't part of the plan, but he didn't want Phoenix to know that—he didn't want to appear less in control than he did already.

"You finish your business and finish it soon," said Cocteau, "and I'll make sure Spartan gets stuffed back in the freezer. Think of him as a guarantee."

Phoenix smiled thinly. "A guarantee? A guarantee that I get the job done? Is that what you mean? Listen, Ray, I took care of Spartan once before, so don't worry your pointy little head about that. Okay?" Phoenix stood up. "Now we need these guys thawed out fast. The sooner I get what I need, the sooner you get what you want? Got it?"

Cocteau nodded. "Whatever you require."

Inwardly, he cursed Edgar Friendly. That miserable Scrap was the cause of all this damn trouble, and he would pay for that. Pay dearly . . .

Associate Bob scuttled back into the room. "A list is being prepared," he reported obsequiously.

"You see, Phoenix. We are doing everything in our power to accommodate you."

Phoenix nodded. "Good, Ray. That's good. Illuminate."

The lights clicked off, and Phoenix chuckled madly, delighted at even this small piece of mischief.

"Illuminate!" snapped Cocteau—but to his immense surprise the lights did not come back on. "Phoenix, what little game are you playing?"

Phoenix giggled in the dark. "Nah, I reprogrammed it. The password isn't illuminate anymore. It's something else. And I guess you'll have to find out." The door slammed, and Dr. Cocteau and Associate Bob stood alone in the dark.

"What a distasteful fellow," said Associate Bob.

Cocteau had had enough. "Oh shut up, Bob," he snapped.

"Yes, Dr. Cocteau," said Associate Bob meekly.

16

John Spartan expected that Lenina Huxley would be a little standoffish when they met up the next morning. After all, he had committed the unpardonable sin of suggesting an unprotected act of fluid transfer—with touching and kissing and all that good outlawed stuff.

Indeed, Lenina Huxley was all business when they met early the next day at the police cruiser.

"Good morning," said Spartan pleasantly. He was carrying a leather bag over one shoulder.

"Detective," said Lenina Huxley with a nod, chilly and distant.

Spartan walked around the side of the car to the driver's door and got in behind the control panel of the police vehicle.

"What are you doing?"

"I've got to learn how to drive this thing sometime," he said with a shrug.

Lenina Huxley made no objection to his taking over the controls. There were other things she wanted to get across to her new and unorthodox partner. She took a deep breath. "I understand that we are to work together, and I think it better if we agree that the events of yesterday evening are better forgotten," she said solemnly.

"Fine," said Spartan.

But Lenina had more she wanted to get off her chest. "I understand that our ways are alien to you, and that despite my industrious study of your era, I too have failed to bridge the gaps between our two disparate cultures."

"That's okay," said Spartan. From the bag he produced a flawlessly knitted sweater made of bright red wool.

"This is for you," he said, handing it to her. "I had to guess at the size, but it looks about right. It's a peace offering, okay?"

Lenina Huxley had expected a number of responses from Spartan, but this one took her completely by surprise. "What a lovely sweater," she said, holding it against her. "Beautifully made."

Spartan pushed some buttons on the control console, and the car eased into traffic, humming along smoothly. Spartan shook his head. "I don't know what they put in cryo-slush," he said, "but as soon as I thaw out the first thing I want to do is knit. I don't get it."

"You knit very well," said Lenina, giving him a verbal pat on the back.

"I know," he said. "That's what so strange. How

come I know what a zipper foot is, a shuttle, hook and bobbin, petit point. I could weave a throw rug right now with my eyes closed.''

Huxley laughed. This was one mystery she could resolve. ''It was your rehab training,'' she said.

Spartan shot her a look ''My what?''

''Your rehab training. For each inmate a computer designs a program that draws on innate skills of the cryo-prisoner. It takes a scan of your genetic disposition and assigns a skill or a trade based on your unique makeup. It really is quite ingenious.''

''Really,'' said Spartan, unimpressed.

''Yes,'' said Lenina with a nod. ''Once it has decided your natural predisposition, it implants the knowledge and desire to carry out whatever training was assigned. The computer has created a master seamstress in you, John Spartan.''

''I'm a seamstress?'' said Spartan, dumbfounded. ''Seamstress. That's just great.'' He turned toward Lenina. ''How come I come out of cryo-prison and I'm Betsy fucking Ross.''

''Knitting is a valuable skill,'' said Lenina as primly as a schoolmarm. ''And research shows that knitting can reduce heart rate, stress levels, and high blood pressure.''

''That's not the point,'' said Spartan. ''Phoenix comes out of prison, and he can access computers, operate all vehicles, find the locations of every damn thing in the city—and he's three times stronger than when he went in. Now, would you care to tell me what kind of rehab program that might be?''

''I don't know,'' said Lenina. ''I cannot explain it.''

"Well, could you get me a copy of that program? Let's see who juiced this guy up."

Lenina thought for a moment and then leaned into the computer screen and madly began punching codes. The first three responses were predictable.

"Access denied," cooed the computer voice.

"Drat," said Lenina.

"Drat?" asked Spartan. "That's some pretty strong language you're using."

But Lenina ignored the sarcasm as her hands flew over the keyboard. Spartan smiled as he watched her concentrating on breaking the rules—he was glad to see that even here in the future cops were still not above stretching the regulations to the edge of the unlawful.

The computer denied Lenina access three more times, each refusal making her angrier—"drat" actually became "damn"—and more determined to succeed in cracking the code.

By a series of subterfuges and outright lies—at one point she identified herself as none other than Chief George Earle—Lenina did manage to get around the security system.

The computer emitted a high-pitched shriek that made Lenina and Spartan jump.

"What the hell is that?"

Lenina was smiling, but Spartan could see that her dark eyes were tinged with fear. "That's the warning. I've entered an ultrasecure zone. The computer will check every possible access code in the next few seconds. If I've done this correctly, we'll be admitted to the restricted files."

Abruptly, the mechanized scream ceased. The alarm signal was replaced by a calm, female voice.

"Enter subject name."

Lenina typed fast. The computer hesitated for a moment as if it couldn't quite believe that anyone had access to the rehab file of Simon Phoenix. But the codes checked out, and a second later the brain spewed out information.

"Phoenix, Simon," said the computer. "Rehabilitation skills: urban combat, computer override authorization, violence, adept murder-death-kill dexterity."

Lenina Huxley was shocked; she could only stare at the screen, dumbfounded. "But . . . there must be some mistake. This isn't a proper rehab program."

"No kidding," said Spartan.

"These skills were abolished decades ago." She looked at Spartan, her eyes wide. "The Mayor-Gov would never allow this kind of thing."

"Oh, no," said Spartan. "He'd be shocked, I'm sure, if he knew what kind of faculties his precious cryo-prison was teaching the bad guys."

"Well, he would," protested Lenina. "This kind of program would create a . . . a monster."

"Create?" said Spartan. "They started with a monster. All they managed to do with this program was make a new improved, state-of-the-art monster."

"But why?" demanded Huxley. "What would be the point of formulating something—someone—so horrible?"

Spartan shook his head. "Don't know why," he said, "but I can guess who. Who develops these programs?"

"All programming is done by Cocteau Industries,

of course," Lenina replied. "But why would Mayor-Gov Cocteau want to release such a brute savage into our midst? It would counter everything he has ever tried to do. Everything he stands for. It would destroy his dream."

"That's a good question," said Spartan. "Let's go ask him." He threw the police car into a rubber-burning one-hundred-and-eighty-degree turn, the kind of spectacular traffic-stopping stratagem unseen in the city since the bad old days of the violent nineties.

He cut across three lanes of traffic, jumped a bright green grass divider, and slammed onto the freeway lane going back the way they came. A dozen cars on the lane came to screeching halts, and the drivers immediately began hunting for the horns on their cars. They never used them so they weren't quite sure where they were located.

"John Spartan!" squawked Lenina holding on for all she was worth. "What are you doing?"

"Turning around."

"That is not the approved manner," she said sternly.

But Spartan could tell that she was a little breathless with excitement and secretly pleased with the daring maneuver on San Angeles's normally serene highways.

She was less pleased with the next phase of Spartan's audacious plan.

"You are intending to put a question directly to Mayor-Gov Dr. Raymond Cocteau?" she asked in disbelief.

Spartan nodded. "That's right."

"No, John Spartan. You can't accuse the savior

of the city of a thing like that! You can't charge him with being connected to a multimurder-death-killer like Simon Phoenix. It would be . . . it would be rude.''

Spartan almost winced. Police work had come to a pretty sorry state when a cop was afraid to ask a question of a suspect because to do so would be rude.

"Rude?" he said. "Don't worry about rude. I'll be subtle. I'm good at subtle.''

Lenina looked less than reassured. Nothing she had seen in John Spartan suggested subtlety—except, perhaps, for the red sweater, and he was the first to admit that knitting it had flown in the face of his true nature.

Associate Bob did not look happy to see John Spartan as the two cops came barging into Dr. Cocteau's outer office.

"Where's Cocteau?" asked Spartan gruffly. Lenina Huxley had never been in the Holy of Holies before—the Mayor-Gov's suite of offices—and she shrunk back in embarrassment, mortified by John Spartan's lack of respect for the sacred place.

Associate Bob was less flustered. Like a well-trained guard dog Associate Bob's first instinct was to deny all access to the master, and both cops could see that Cocteau's assistant was going to be tenacious about letting them in.

"I am ever so sorry, John Spartan," said Associate Bob unctuously. "Dr. Raymond Cocteau is not available for your unannounced visit. I don't think I can access him at this time." He turned back to his computer screen. "Be well."

John Spartan decided to cut right to the chase.

He grabbed Associate Bob by the throat and slammed him against one of the eight vid screens that surrounded his desk.

"Think again."

Associate Bob had never been choked before, and he found the sensation most unpleasant. More frightening, though, was the look in Spartan's eyes. Cocteau's assistant realized that the choke hold would only get tighter the longer he resisted. So *he* cut to the chase. What was the point of experiencing a great deal of pain if he was going to end up giving in eventually.

"I will give my utmost efforts to securing you an appointment with the Mayor-Gov immediately, sir."

"I thought you'd see it my way," said Spartan, shoving the man back in his chair. Associate Bob dropped to his computer keyboard and he typed frantically for a moment or two.

"Oh, wonder of wonders," said Associate Bob breathlessly, "I have located the Mayor-Gov on Fiber-Op in the main conference room."

"Isn't that a stroke of luck," said Spartan.

"Detective Spartan," whispered Lenina Huxley. "Please! Remember where you are!"

Spartan did not have time to reply. Cocteau's always tranquil face appeared on all eight screens at once.

"Mellow apologies for my lack of physical disposition, Detective," he said condescendingly. But I do have an entire city-gov to run."

Lenina stepped up to the screen. "Mellow greetings, Mayor-Gov. We apologize for interrupting your busy day, but John Spartan and I have—"

Spartan had no time to waste on pleasantries. "Run this," he snarled. "*You* programmed Phoenix's rehab to turn him into a bigger, better terrorist. And I don't think his escape was an accident either."

Lenina rolled her eyes. "This is very subtle, John Spartan. *Very* subtle."

Cocteau's face was like a smooth mask, and he stared at the two cops with his weird hypnotic sincerity.

"Well," he said very slowly. "Let's take a look at the file, shall we? Associate Bob, Simon Phoenix's rehabilitation encoding. Now."

"Yes, Mayor-Gov." The information began scrolling onto the screen as the cool female voice read off the information.

"Phoenix, Simon," she said. "Rehabilitation skills: decorative gardening, retail floral arrangements, in-home horticulture, ornamental and fancy gift wraps . . ."

Cocteau continued to smile. "What are you speaking of, Detective? My only interest in Simon Phoenix was to assist in the creation of an expert florist."

"Florist?" said Spartan. "Phoenix wouldn't know a prickly pear from a pair of pricks."

"And I remind you, John Spartan, you did not know how to knit before cryo-rehab."

Spartan was getting nowhere fast. He decided to accelerate the pace a little. He pulled the Beretta stolen from the museum out of his pocket and blasted out three of the eight screens. Associate Bob dove for cover. Lenina Huxley stared in disbelief. But Raymond Cocteau had not moved a muscle.

"Let's try again, Cocteau. Another line of questioning if you don't mind."

"I am at your service, Detective."

"Outside the museum, why didn't Phoenix blow your brains out?" Spartan demanded.

Cocteau shrugged. "I was no threat to him, perhaps? I honestly do not know. Does it matter?"

"It matters," said Spartan. "You don't have to be a threat to Phoenix to end up dead, Doc. I saw the security discs—Phoenix had plenty of time to think about where to put the hole in your head."

"John Spartan," retorted Cocteau, "this display of barbaric behavior was not acceptable even in your time."

Spartan fired three more times and three more vid screens shattered. Associate Bob's nerves short-circuited, and he fainted dead away.

"When a man like Phoenix has a gun to your head, ten seconds is nine and a half seconds longer than you live."

"Not everyone is as eager as you to resort to violence to solve all the difficulties in life," said Cocteau dreamily. "Even now I am beginning to wonder if the chaos in the museum was the result of Mr. Phoenix's presence or your own. It seems reasonable to assume—"

He stopped suddenly. The warm nose of the Baretta was now pressed against the back of his skull. Spartan had lost patience with talking to the Mayor-Gov by vid screen. He had walked down the corridor and straight into conference room.

"It is unreasonable to assume, shithead" said

Spartan, "that you can control this guy. Trust me . . . you can't."

Cocteau was unfazed. "Is there something specific you plan to do with that archaic device?"

Spartan lowered the gun. He would like to have taken the smug expression off Cocteau's placid face, but the Mayor-Gov was the key to the whole puzzle.

Cocteau smiled. "I didn't think so. Detective, the only thing I haven't got under control is *you*. But that can be solved. You, my Cro-Magnon friend, are dead. Your family is dead. Your past is dead. Dead things can't affect the living."

"Don't bet on it," said Spartan.

The Mayor-Gov sighed, as if he was deathly bored with Spartan's performance. "I suggest you enjoy your moment of prehistoric bravado, because after you leave here, it's all over for you. Like everything else in your life."

Cocteau turned and gestured to Huxley, like a diner summoning a waiter. "Officer, return this man to cryo-stasis immediately. Be well."

Spartan looked at him a long moment. "Be fucked."

Lenina Huxley recoiled in horror, while the conference room morality box burped angrily.

"John Spartan—" was about as far as it got. Spartan raised the gun and blasted the box off the wall. But his eyes never left Cocteau.

17

It looked like Spartan would go quietly. Lenina Huxley escorted him back to the cruiser and was relieved to see that Alfredo Garcia had joined her as backup in the arrest of John Spartan.

"I am commanded to place you under arrest, John Spartan," said Lenina Huxley, feeling a trifle self-conscious.

"Aren't you gonna read me my rights?" said Spartan.

"Your what?" asked Alfredo Garcia.

"Forget it," said Spartan, getting into the cruiser. "Let's go."

They drove in silence for a while, and Lenina Huxley had the feeling that right at that moment John Spartan probably did not care if he lived or died. Dr. Cocteau's words had been cruel, and

Lenina was sure that Spartan was dwelling on one thought exclusively.

"Your family is dead," Cocteau had said. "Your past is dead."

To Spartan that meant that he really only had one thing to live for, revenge.

If he allowed himself to be taken into custody, Simon Phoenix would be free to carry out his criminal plan. John Spartan couldn't allow that.

"Stop the car!" he said suddenly.

Garcia was driving and he looked alarmed. "What?"

"I said stop the car!" The car screeched to a halt at the intersection of Wilshire and Santa Monica. All signs of Simon Phoenix's murderous mayhem of the day before had been carefully cleared away.

John Spartan climbed out of the police cruiser and marched over to a ventilation duct set flush in the roadway. He ripped up one of the steel planks, a rush of hot air blasting out of the ground.

"What are you doing?" demanded Lenina.

"Escaping," said Spartan. He pulled another steel slat from the sticky asphalt.

Lenina shook her head. "No, no, you can't do that. We have to escort you to the cryo-prison. Those are my orders. You wouldn't want me to disobey a direct order, would you."

Spartan paused and stared deep into her eyes. "Look, you do what you gotta do, but I know what I gotta do," he said angrily. "My only chance is to nail this asshole and put him back on ice—or that's where I'm gonna be." The muscles in his neck appeared to clench and unclench like steel cables.

"Enhance your calm, John Spartan," said Garcia trying to pacify his prisoner. "Don't mega-stress."

Spartan ripped another bar from the grate and threw it away. "I *like* mega-stress. I've had it with enhancing my calm! I am going to locate this psycho Phoenix and enhance *his* calm. Got it?"

"Perhaps we should call for backup," Garcia suggested.

Lenina shook her head. "Enhance *your* calm, Alfredo Garcia," she said.

"It's very difficult."

Spartan had opened a wide hole in the ground and was working to make it extensive enough for him to squeeze through. "And I'll tell you something else; when I'm done with Phoenix, I'm going to turn my attention to that fruitloop Cocteau." The gap was big enough now, and he was preparing to drop down into the sewer, but he paused.

"Look," he said, "you don't have to come with me. I can do this alone."

Garcia nodded quickly. "He's right, Lenina Huxley, we have very good careers."

Huxley could not believe that things had become so serious. "John Spartan, do you realize what you're doing? That you're going on the sheep?"

Spartan looked at her, his eyes narrowing. "On the sheep? It's the lam. I'm going *on the lam*."

"Oh," said Huxley, coloring slightly.

Garcia was genuinely scared—but he didn't know which frightened him more: the wrath of the Mayor-Gov or the scorn of John Spartan.

"Even if Simon Phoenix was programmed to escape," he asked nervously, "even if he has the power to extinguish life and steal contraband weapons, pray tell why you are proceeding down there? To the depths of the Wasteland.''

"That's simple.'' Spartan put his foot on the first rung of the ladder set in the cement wall of the tunnel. "The reason the city-wide manhunt didn't work was because Phoenix was down in the one place where you can't monitor. Where you're afraid to go. A place you just don't give a shit about.''

Alfredo Garcia shot a sidelong glance into the dark hole and swallowed nervously. Every single thing Spartan had said about the Wasteland was absolutely true.

"Look,'' said John Spartan. "I'm going down there, I'm gonna find Phoenix, and I'm gonna put him in the hurt locker. You wanna come with me or you want to arrest me?''

Lenina Huxley considered her alternatives for a almost a second. "Okay,'' she said with a smile. "I'm with you. Let's go blow this guy.''

Spartan winced. "That's 'blow this guy away,'" he said.

Lenina Huxley shrugged. "Whatever.''

It turned out that not all pieces of San Angeles Police Department equipment were as useless as the stun batons. Officers were equipped with nifty flashlights called lightwands, and three of them carried by Spartan, Huxley, and Garcia lit up the wide sewer pipe.

The bright light didn't make Alfredo Garcia feel any less nervous, and he shivered in the wind that moaned eerily through the tunnel. "My dog's better than your dog," he sang nervously. "My dog's better than yours . . . dog's better 'cause he . . .''

Spartan stopped and stared at him. "Are you singing?"

Garcia flinched. "I'm sorry, when I'm nervous I find it helpful to sing an oldie. I . . . sorry."

They continued to creep forward until they reached a rusty hatch, a sealing wheel in the center of the corroded metal.

"This looks like the way in," said Spartan. He seized hold of the wheel and turned it, fighting with the stiff metal until the lock broke and the hatch swung on its ancient hinges.

The three police officers stepped from the dank sewer pipe and straight into a different world.

The Wasteland was a parallel cosmos, an environment deep beneath the city of San Angeles, but it could not have been more different.

First of all, the Wasteland was not a wasteland. It was bustling community—the narrow thoroughfare in which the cops found themselves was crowded and busy. There were dwellings everywhere, people living in every nook and cranny of the subterranean city.

Everywhere they looked they saw evidence of human habitation. Tents and shacks, lean-tos, shanties, and huts were crammed into every conceivable space. The living area looked like an old Third World refugee camp.

The marketplace was like a souk, a collection of stalls crammed with the junk and discards of the city above. The Wasteland was the underbelly of San Angeles, the underground universe lit by strand after strand of dim light bulbs encased in construction cages, old neon advertising signs, and streetlights salvaged or stolen from the metropolis overhead.

The light shone on an intersection of a tangle of old conduits that had once carried water and telephone cables, mixed with a disused subway tunnel and what appeared to be a natural cavern. On closer inspection, Spartan realized that the cavern was, in fact, a man-made excavation.

The Scraps had burrowed into a fifty-year-old sanitary landfill dump, harvesting the useful trash of a distant time. As the miners worked their way into the rubbish, they cleared more room for the ever-expanding Scrap population.

The air was lively with the sounds of people talking—English, Spanish, a babble of a dozen Asian languages—as well as the smells of cooking fires and sweat. It was different from the antiseptic, sterile air of San Angeles. This place was poor and dirty, but it was alive and vital.

The people were dressed in rags and castoffs and looked thin and malnourished. But they didn't have the phony plastic smiles of the San Angelenos, and they looked at the three police officers without fear. A few young men recognized Spartan from the battle in front of the Taco Bell the night before, but now they did not shrink back. They were in their own habitat and would fight to defend it.

Already the buzz was starting that there were strangers in the Wasteland, but Spartan and his two colleagues did not notice. They were still gazing at this strange underground world.

Children played in the streets, and mothers nursed babies at their breasts. Old men and women looked as if they had lived their whole lives in this strange environment.

Spartan liked it down in the Wasteland. "So," he asked Lenina and Alfredo, "these are the terrifying savages that threaten your happy city?"

Huxley's eyes were wide with wonder. "I had no idea . . ." she gasped. "We've always been told the only people down here were thugs and hooligans . . . I can't believe that there are women and children here . . ."

But Spartan was not paying attention. He was sniffing the air and smiling. Alfredo Garcia had gotten a whiff of the same smell and was looking distinctly nauseated.

"What is that emanation?" Garcia tried to talk and hold his breath at the same time.

Spartan grinned. "Oh, yeah . . . yeah. I know that smell." A thirty-six-year memory came flooding back. He slapped Garcia on the back. "*That* emanation, old buddy, is the smell of cooking meat!"

Alfredo swallowed hard to keep his kelp-and-yeast breakfast from coming up.

The three police officers drifted toward a large, square hole cut in a sewer wall in front of which an old woman tended to some meat and buns cooking on a makeshift grill. Behind her a number of Scraps were in the room beyond the fires. They were sitting in ratty old armchairs, and to Lenina Huxley's horror they were smoking cigarettes.

Spartan looked as if he had died and gone to heaven. "Thank God! Real burgers . . ." He turned to the Scraps. "Got any smokes? Marlboros?"

Now it was Lenina Huxley's turn to look nause-ated. "I think I'm going to be sick."

John Spartan was salivating, and he was desper-ate for some cholesterol and nicotine. He snatched Lenina's watch off her wrist and offered it to the old woman. She examined it and smiled.

"Buenos dias, señor," she said. She flipped a meat patty onto some bread, doused it with a red-dish brown sauce, and passed it to Spartan, along with a grease-stained cigarette.

He cadged a light from the grill and sucked the smoke into his lungs, exhaling with a satisfied groan. Then he chomped down on the burger, al-most devouring the food in a couple of great big bites.

The old woman offered a burger to Garcia. Al-fredo turned away. "No . . . no, thank you." He patted his stomach. "Full. Couldn't eat a mouth-ful." He also could hardly stand to watch John Spartan, who was alternating chewing and smoking like a unhealthy machine.

"I love that special sauce," he said deliriously. "This tastes great."

Huxley fought her squeamishness. "Just don't ask where the meat comes from."

"Come from? What do you mean? Where else do burgers come from? From cows, right?"

Huxley laughed. "Did you see any cows on our way down here, Detective?"

Spartan had only one bite of his hamburger left, and he stared at it, trying to determine the origin of the tasty meat. He turned to the old woman.

"De que este carne?" he asked in his best—but not very good—Spanish.

The old woman laughed, throwing a veined old hand in front of her mouth to hide her broken teeth. "Es de rata, señor. Muy, muy sabroso!"

Spartan paused a moment, a very thoughtful look on his face. He gazed at the burger. "Rat burgers," he said quietly, thinking it over. "I'm eating a rat burger."

"Ugh," said Lenina Huxley.

Alfredo Garcia was on the verge of losing his breakfast; he nervously hopped from one foot to another and tried to take shallow breaths to avoid smelling the roasting meats.

Spartan shrugged and then popped the last piece of the burger into his mouth.

"Not bad," he said, winking at the old woman, "best damn burger I ever had. Muy bien, señora."

The rat burger vendor nodded. "Gracias, señor." She turned to Huxley, offering her a rat burger. "Señorita?"

Lenina was horror-struck. "No . . . No thanks."

Spartan shook his head. "Hey, take it. It's on the house."

"Never!"

John Spartan couldn't understand it. "You should never look a gift rat in the mouth."

18

The inhabitants of the Wasteland had learned to make the most of their meager natural resources. Using odd pieces of scrap metal filched from the upper world or harvested from the underground landfill refuse mine, along with discarded engine parts powered by electricity filched from the San Angeles generator nets, they had created an engine workshop deep in the interior of the caverns.

Surrounding the improvised workshop were the cadavers of a score of wrecked automobiles, and a number of Scraps were working on them, cannibalizing the machines that were beyond saving to make jerry-rigged vehicles that were rusty and dented—but they looked liked they worked. And Spartan saw, to his delight, that they were *real* cars, good old-fashioned, fossil-fuel-burning, polluting gas guzzlers.

But nothing was thrown away in the Wasteland. The few hulks that had been stripped to their bare frames had been patched and converted into tiny dwelling places, single unit residences which could accommodate one or possibly two people.

The one car in the cavern that had not been touched by the industrious mechanics was a bright red, pristine muscle car from the 1970s. In the nineteen nineties it had been considered a thoroughbred. Now it was a classic.

Spartan walked over to it and touched the butter soft red paint. "Well," he said nostalgically, "would you look at this baby."

Huxley nodded. "A 1970 Oldsmobile Cutlass 442 with a 455-cubic-inch engine, radial tires, and bucket seats. Four-four-two stands for four barrel carbs, four on the floor, two bucket seats. And this model is seriously beyond the standard package."

Spartan looked at her approvingly. "Huxley, I'm very impressed."

"I studied the past."

The cold snout of a large caliber handgun poked into Spartan's back.

"That's funny. I studied the past, too," said a voice behind him. It was Edgar Friendly and his collection of Scrap fighters. Spartan looked around. They all had guns.

"You got balls, cop," said Friendly. "Coming down here after the show you put on last night."

Lenina Huxley did her best to assert control. After all, she was a sworn officer of the law. "We're looking for a murder-death-killer," she said, trying to sound as tough as possible. "Can you help? Or just bully us with those primitive weapons?"

Friendly took the gun off Spartan just long enough to fire the weapon once, blowing a hole in the side of one of the abandoned cars. The noise was deafening, and the heat and smoke of the explosion made the dank air acrid and choking. Alfredo Garcia almost dropped to the floor in fright.

Lenina did her best not to flinch, to keep up her tough cop act. "Well, maybe they're not so primitive."

Edgar Friendly was not taken in by the performance. "Not funny, not smart," he snarled at her. Then he whipped around and stuffed the heavy revolver right into Spartan's face, as if the Scraps leader intended to blast a slug into the cop's left nostril.

"So?" he asked. "I guess you came down here to take me in. I don't think so."

"You will submit to the law," said Huxley.

Friendly shook his head. "Guess what? Not happening. You can tell Cocteau to kiss my ass."

Alfredo Garcia inhaled sharply. He had never heard obscenity and the Mayor-Gov's name mentioned in the same breath.

Edgar Friendly was delighted with the shock effect of his words. "Yeah, that's right. His rules don't apply down here. Fuck him! Tell him it's going to take an army of assholes to get rid of me."

"Why do you say these things?" demanded Huxley. "Why do you want to live like this?"

"'Cause I don't give a shit," he said. "Lady, I got nothing to lose. And you can also tell your precious master—"

Spartan had long ago had his fill of tough talk. He pushed the gun out of his face. It was obvious to him that the Scraps leader had no intention of using it—if he had, why would he have spent the last five minutes giving them obscene and defiant messages to carry back to Dr. Cocteau.

"Look pal," said Spartan. "I don't want to piss on your parade, but I don't even know who the hell you are. Let alone want to take you anywhere. Stay here. Eat rat. Be well. And for the record, Cocteau *is* an asshole." Spartan started stalking away, back down the main street of the Wasteland.

Friendly looked puzzled. He never imagined that he would hear a man dressed in the uniform of the San Angeles Police Department talk with such disrespect of the exalted leader of the city above.

"Wait. Wait. Wait. Whoa!"

Spartan stopped. "Yeah?"

Friendly peered at him. "Just what is it you want, anyway? What did you come down here for if it wasn't for me? Last night, at the Taco Bell, you were ready to kill everybody."

"That was last night. You can bust up every Taco Bell in the whole goddamn city for all I care." Spartan turned and walked back toward Friendly a step or two. "I got a few questions. What I really came down here for was a few answers."

Suddenly, all of the Scraps cocked their weapons and aimed them at the three cops.

"But if it's a bad time for questions," said Alfredo Garcia, "we could always come back later."

"It's always a bad time for questions down here," said Friendly.

Spartan noticed something he hadn't seen before.

There was graffiti spray painted on the cavern walls. I HATE SAN ANGELES! screamed one piece of wall writing. SUCK MY COCTEAU proclaimed another.

Spartan smiled wryly. "Yeah," he said, as if suddenly everything made sense. "I guess you weren't really part of Cocteau's plan."

Friendly's face darkened, and cold anger shone in his eyes. "I don't know what planet you're from, mister. But if you ask me, greed is no *plan*. Lying is no *plan*. Neither is abuse of power."

"What is his plan then?" asked Spartan.

Friendly's laugh was hollow. "That's simple. The plan is everyone who doesn't agree with him has got to leave. Get with the Cocteau program or get the hell out."

"And that's why you're down here?"

Friendly nodded vehemently. "You got that right. See—according to Cocteau's plan, I'm the enemy. The good doctor thinks I'm dangerous."

Out of the corner of his eye Friendly saw Huxley staring at him, or rather, at the gun he held. The Scraps leader turned on her.

"Dangerous—that's right. But not because of this." He waved the gun under her nose. "No, dangerous for another more deadly reason."

"What's that?" asked Lenina Huxley.

"I like to think. I like to read. I'm into freedom of speech and freedom of choice."

"Noble of you," said Spartan.

"Fuck noble," Friendly shot back. "The hell with it. I'm the kind of guy who wants to walk into a titty bar at three in the morning and order a double shot of Jack Daniel's on the rocks with a cold Heineken chaser."

Spartan nodded. "Who said that wasn't noble?"

Friendly was on a roll and ignored him, consumed with his vision of how the world *should* be. "I wanna sit in a greasy spoon and wonder, gee, should I have the T-bone steak or should I have the jumbo rack of barbecued ribs with a side order of gravy fries. I want *high cholesterol*!" His voice echoed off the steel of the cars and stone walls.

Lenina Huxley and Alfredo Garcia listened, amazement showing on their faces.

But Friendly was far from done. The pent-up frustration flowed out him, hot, like molten lava. "I want to eat bacon and butter and cheese. I want to smoke a Cuban cigar the size of Cincinnati. I want to spit and fart and fuck all night. I've seen the future, pal, and I know what it is."

"Tell me," said Spartan.

"It ain't pretty," Friendly snarled. "It's a forty-seven-year-old virgin sitting around in his beige pajamas, drinking a banana broccoli shake and singing 'I wish I was an Oscar Meyer wiener.' That's what it is."

"Ugly," agreed Spartan.

"Damn right. You live up top, you live the way Cocteau wants you to. *What* he wants, *when* he wants, how he wants . . . Your only choice is to come down here, maybe to starve to death . . ." Friendly's voice was calmer now, like distant thunder after a storm.

"Brave new world, huh, cop?" he said quietly. Then he stuffed his weapon in his pocket. Following their leader's example, the rest of his band did the same thing.

"Maybe the time has come for you to lead these people out of here," said Spartan.

Friendly shook his head. "I'm no leader," he said. "I do what I have to do. Sometimes people come along with me." He shrugged. "I'm not the only one who thinks this way."

Spartan refused to let it go at that. Revolutions had grown from smaller, weaker seeds. "Look around you," he said. "You got something worth doing, people who want to do it with you, and you're willing to risk your own ass. That's what makes you a leader. You have a vision."

Friendly laughed and shook his head. "Oh yeah, I got vision. I got a vision all right. I got a vision of closing down this anal little world, burying Cocteau up to his neck in sewage, and let him think his happy, happy thoughts forever."

"Yeah," said one of the Scraps. "Get him!"

Alfredo Garcia looked as if he was about to faint. He wondered, not for the first time, if he was going to get out of this hellhole alive.

"Well," said Spartan, "like I said. You've got the noble ideas. The problem is, I got the bad news . . ."

"Which is?" said Friendly.

"Cocteau wants to kill you."

The Wasteland was big enough to hide in, but you didn't have to hide if you didn't want to, particularly if you looked like Simon Phoenix and his company of recently thawed killers. They swaggered through the dirty side streets of the Wasteland and straight into the first broken-down bar they found.

There were six in Phoenix's merry band of killers, with cute killer-type names: Beppo, Kodo, Danzig, and Elvin. And some perfectly normal ones: Adam and Francis.

They settled at a table in the deepest, darkest recesses of the bar and ordered a pitcher of the deadly home-brewed white lightning. Too much of the rotgut and you could go blind. But a couple of shots and you could feel pretty mellow.

Phoenix called his board of assassins to order. "Gentlemen, let's review. It's the year 2032. That's two oh three two, as in the twenty-first century."

"No shit," said Beppo. "What's it like?"

Phoenix cackled. "That's the beauty part, Beppo. The world upstairs is a pussy-whipped Brady Bunch version of itself, and all we gotta do to run the whole place is kill this guy named Raymond, who put it all together."

"Piece of cake," said Kodo.

"Right," agreed Phoenix. "And the extra added bonus, you get to kill the man who put most of us in the freezer, your pal and mine, John Spartan."

"That asshole," said Francis.

"The same," said Phoenix. "This is the plan. Adam, you can crush him. Kodo, you can slash him. And the rest of you can rape, pillage, loot, and all the fun things you can remember."

"Great!" said Elvin and Danzig simultaneously.

"This place is going to be like a theme park," said Phoenix. "But with our kind of themes. So let's drink up and get busy with the plan."

Adam, however, remained fixed on one point. "You sure we get to kill John Spartan?"

"Over and over and over, if that's your pleasure."

"It is."

"Good." He raised his beaker of rotgut. "Salud!"

1 9

News of the San Angeles Police interlopers in the Wasteland had spread through the Scraps in the underground city, and a crowd of onlookers had gathered to hear what they had to say. On the edge of the throng stood a middle-aged woman, thin and tall, a sadness in her dark eyes that detracted slightly from her still fresh good looks. As Friendly talked to Spartan, she began edging through the crowd, gradually working her way closer to the intruders.

The information that Cocteau wanted him dead didn't seem to faze Edgar Friendly all that much. He merely shrugged his shoulders and looked unconcerned.

"And you're the guy, right? Cocteau got you from somewhere to come down here and ice me.

Now I got the feeling that you aren't going to do that. So, why should I be worried?"

Spartan nodded. "That's right. It's not me you have to worry about. I got out of the freezer by accident. The guy you should be having nightmares about got out on purpose. His name is Simon Phoenix."

Lenina Huxley and Alfredo Garcia jumped at the mention of the name.

"John Spartan," said Alfredo Garcia. "I must protest! It has been reported that Simon Phoenix affected his own unauthorized release from X23-1. It resulted in no less than four murder-death-kills and—"

"You can believe that if you want, but your pal Cocteau programmed Phoenix to be a fucking walking slaughterhouse and then turned him loose to go after our pal here."

"Impossible," said Garcia flatly.

But Lenina was not so sure. "It is a curious conclusion you have deduced here, John Spartan, but I can find no fault in your logic."

"No fault?" said Alfredo Garcia. "I cannot believe that you would say such a thing."

"Simon Phoenix would be the perfect weapon," explained Lenina Huxley. "A murder-death-killer admirably suited to the savage nether regions in which we stand."

"The Mayor-Gov has no need of weapons," grumbled Alfredo Garcia. "It is one of the governing tenets of our society."

"You need 'em down here," said Spartan.

Friendly shook his head. "You mean they thawed this guy out to kill me? I'm flattered."

"Don't be flattered," Spartan growled. "Be frightened. This guy's a fucking nightmare . . . What did you do to piss Cocteau off this much anyhow."

"We've tapped into the water and power supply," Friendly responded. "We've stolen food and disrupted communications, fermented discontent. Oh, yeah. I forgot. And we've put up malicious slogans wherever we can. That's kind of what we're best at." Spartan could tell that Friendly didn't rate his own chances against Phoenix all that high.

He tried to reassure the leader of the Scraps. "It sounds like you're off to a good start."

"As lawbreakers we're kinda amateurs."

"Listen," said Spartan, "when the laws are wrong, men have to take it upon themselves to change them."

Lenina Huxley still had reflexes that would not die. "John Spartan, you must uphold the law."

"Depends on what they are," he said simply. "And who makes them."

"Now it's your turn to be noble," said Friendly.

"I don't know about that," Spartan answered. "But I do know the next time you want to go shopping and trash a Taco Bell, I'm not going to get in your way."

"That's good to know."

Just then, the middle-aged woman stepped out of the crowd and looked at John Spartan closely.

"You are John Spartan?" she asked.

"That's right."

But she had to be sure. "The Demolition Man, John Spartan," she asked urgently. "*That* John Spartan?"

Spartan looked at the woman quizzically, as if

trying to look beyond the wrinkles and the graying hair. "Do I know you?"

The woman smiled and blinked back the tears in her eyes. "You did. A long time ago." She took a step closer. "You made me a promise once."

Spartan felt a wave of raw, unsorted, inchoate emotion. "Yeah," he said. "That's right." He gazed at the woman and suddenly felt light-headed and shaken.

"You're Katie?" he asked.

Katie Spartan's voice was low, heavy with emotion. "Yeah. I'm Katie."

"You're my daughter," he said, exhaling heavily.

Katherine laughed nervously, unsure of what to do next. "Yeah, I'm your daughter . . . And I'm older than you are . . . I don't know what to say." Suddenly, her face fell. "Mom . . . she's not . . ." She struggled for words, trying to pull together her unraveling emotions. "I'm afraid Mom is . . ."

"I know," said Spartan. "I know what happened to her."

Spartan stumbled forward, unsteady on his feet, and pulled his daughter to him, holding her in a tentative hug. Katherine Spartan closed her eyes, as if she could not quite believe what was happening.

Edgar Friendly, too, was having a certain amount of trouble accepting what was going on. "Is this for fucking real?" he asked, looking around.

"Yes," said Garcia adamantly. "Actually it is for fu-fu-u . . . it is for real!"

"Will you two shut up," said Lenina, watching father and daughter, tears in her eyes.

Katie Spartan pulled back from her father and gazed at him. He was transfixed by her.

"I missed . . . I missed everything. Your whole life. I missed your whole life!"

Katherine smiled crookedly. "I know . . . it's okay. You're lucky. I was a real bitch as a teenager. I was always getting into trouble. I had a little problem with authority. Sound familiar?"

John Spartan grinned and stroked his daughter's hair. "That sounds great. I'm proud of you."

"Proud of me?" Katherine exclaimed. "How can you be proud of me? You barely knew me."

"You're down here, aren't you," said Spartan. "You're down here fighting and not groveling butt up there."

"It's in the genes."

"Whatever the reason, that's more than enough to make your old dad proud."

"Old? *I'm* the one who's old."

"Forget that. Tell me everything. I want to know everything about you."

"Everything?" Katherine laughed happily. "Everything, all at once?"

It seemed impossible to Lenina Huxley, but the big grin on John Spartan's face grew wider and happier. He kissed his daughter on the forehead and then held her out at arms' length, just staring at her with that big, bright smile on his face.

"Yes!" he shouted. "Everything. Absolutely everything. Start where I left off. You were six . . ."

"Six? I can't believe I was ever six. Lot of miles on my tires now."

"Hey, I don't want to hear that kind of talk."

Alfredo Garcia was less than enthralled with the

touching scene of a father reunited with his daughter. He tapped Spartan on the shoulder. "Spartan?"

"I'm busy," said Spartan.

But Garcia persisted. "Spartan. I really think—"

Spartan managed to tear himself away from his daughter for a second. "What!"

But Garcia could only point. Spartan followed the line of Garcia's gaze and saw, standing in the middle of the crowd, about forty feet away, Simon Phoenix and his murderous colleagues. The AcMag was in his hand. Spartan's smile faded fast.

A wild look lit Phoenix's eyes, and a grin split his face. It was as if the criminal had picked up Spartan's smile and put it on.

"You know, I musta done something right in a previous life to be this lucky . . ." He thought for a moment. "Don't know what it coulda been, of course . . ."

Then he fired.

Spartan had less than a second to throw himself on Katherine and drag her to ground, shielding her body with his own.

"Get down!" he roared.

Everything seemed to happen simultaneously. The AcMag settled on a rusting hulk of a Chevy, and it burst into flame. Garcia and Huxley and the Scraps fast enough dove for cover.

A pair of rebels did not make it to safety. The two men erupted in twin balls of flame as the AcMag landed on them, their anguished death screams shredding the air around them.

"Two for the price of one," shrieked Phoenix,

still delighted with the AcMag's deadly, devastating performance.

The cryo-cons fanned out around their maniac leader, blasting away with all manner of weapons. Scraps dropped in a volley of bullets, cutting down rebels and innocent bystanders alike as the wind of murderous lead sliced through bone and flesh. The air was alive with the screams and groans of the dying.

Simon Phoenix's sudden, deadly arrival had caught Spartan completely unaware, and he cursed himself for dropping his guard. In the few seconds it took him to regroup and react, half a dozen Scraps had died.

Spartan hardly noticed that he was pinned under a fallen piece of car body. He growled, threw the sheet metal aside, and jumped to his feet. The Baretta appeared in his hand and he fired rapidly, dropping one of the thugs with a perfect shot slapped right into his forehead.

Suddenly, Spartan wasn't alone. Edgar Friendly had jumped up and was returning fire with his big old revolver. Seeing their leader up and fighting back, the other Scraps clambered out of the wreckage and brought their slow, rusty weapons into play.

Phoenix let fly with another vicious blast from the AcMag. The explosion tore through the rickety electrical setup in the work areas, and the lights in the cavern began to flicker and dim, panicking the crowd, who still cowered in niches and holes in the middle of the gunfight.

But it wasn't exclusively a gunfight for long. Neither side was rich in ammunition, and quickly the fighting became hand to hand. That was fine with the goon named Kodo. He liked to kill up close and personal whenever he got the chance—and attacking a bunch of unarmed civilians was right up his alley.

Kodo was slicing and dicing his way through the crowd. Machetes in both hands, he slashed a bloody harvest. He swung one blade and dropped another Scrap, then turned, ready for more. Unfortunately, he spun straight into Spartan, who was waiting for him, a length of heavy pipe in his hands. He cracked Kodo a massive blow to the head and then caught one of the knives as the man headed south. Without hesitation Spartan planted the steel shaft in the tough guy's chest.

''One less,'' said Spartan.

Edgar Friendly had turned out to be a valuable guy to have on one's side in a fight. The instant the firefight erupted, the Scraps leader drew a bead on Beppo, and with about the same consideration he would give to cockroach, pulled the trigger and blew the man away.

He swiveled and saw that Phoenix had the AcMag aimed right at John Spartan. A split second and John Spartan would be carried away in a great sheet of flame. Friendly fired before Phoenix did.

The shot went wide—Edgar Friendly had intended to blow Simon Phoenix's head off—and struck the deadly weapon, the bullet blasting the AcMag out of his hand.

Phoenix had always been a firm believer in the principle of strategic retreat. Unarmed and under the aim of a foe struck him as a good time to take off. He ran down a dark passageway, but Spartan sprinted after him.

Phoenix had no idea where he was going, and when he came to a long, rusty iron catwalk spanning a natural gorge in the depths of the cavern, he did not hesitate. The bridge did not look too solid, but Phoenix had no alternative but to try and escape across it. He darted out onto the rusty girders and felt the beams tremble and quiver as they took his weight.

Spartan was right behind him. He dashed out onto the catwalk, racing after his archenemy. But the combined weight of the two big men was too much for the tired twisted beams, and they gave way with a terrible groan. Spartan and Phoenix were pitched into the void, their frantic hands grabbing for anything to hold on to.

The two men were hanging side by side on the support grid that braced the light track that ran across the chasm. The rebar creaked ominously and threatened to give way at any second.

Spartan and Phoenix hung side by side, the job of killing one another temporarily forgotten with the business of staying alive suddenly so important.

Gingerly, Spartan and Phoenix started inching their way along the pole, hand over hand, trying to pull themselves to safety. The bar sagged alarmingly, and the brittle joints in the iron creaked and flaked.

Sweat poured off Spartan's brow as he crawled centimeter by centimeter toward some kind of safety. Phoenix, on the other hand, like the psycho he was, seemed to be enjoying himself immensely. He laughed so hard he almost tore himself from the bar.

"So, Spartan," said Phoenix, "how do you like the future? A gas, huh?"

"A laugh riot," said Spartan through gritted teeth.

Phoenix continued to babble crazily. "Have you figured out that thing with the seashells yet? What's up with that shit anyway?"

Then, although his voice remained light, amused and delighted with himself, what he actually said next was, to Spartan, absolutely horrifying.

"Hey, you know that thirty something years you spent in the ice box? You remember, more than half your life—the time when your little girl grew up and your wife croaked and you weren't around to do anything about that? Remember that time? All that time you spent learning how to knit while people out here in the real world thought that you were some kind of crazy?"

"Shuttup," snarled Spartan.

Phoenix did not shut up. "Well, I don't know how to tell you this, but it was a complete waste. All thirty years. Remember those bus passengers you blew to pieces, trying to catch me?"

Spartan would never forget them . . .

Phoenix screamed with laughter. "Guess what? They were already dead, pal. Dead before you even touched the building. Cold as a pack of frozen string beans. I went to jail with a thirty-six-year smile— knowing you were right behind me." Phoenix shook his head. "Spartan, if you could *see* the look on your face!"

"You son of a bitch!" roared Spartan.

"Look, I gotta go. It's been good hanging with you. See ya."

Suddenly, Phoenix started rocking back and forth on the bar, gaining momentum—then he launched himself out into space, twisting and arcing, like a diver falling from the high board.

Looking down, Spartan could see Phoenix tumble into a pile of debris fifty feet below. For a moment he stayed very still, and Spartan fired off a fervent prayer that the man had broken his neck—it would be a less satisfying end, but right then Spartan would have taken Phoenix's death any way he could get it.

But it wasn't to be. Phoenix stumbled to his feet and soon vanished into the labyrinthine system of passages that crisscrossed the Wasteland.

Which left Spartan just hanging there. The bar was just about to give, and he tried as hard as he could to pull himself to safety, but the more he fought the more he damaged his spindly support.

Seeing Phoenix escape meant that Spartan could do only one thing. He didn't want to do it, but he didn't have any other choice. With a powerful growl he let go of his handhold and plummeted straight to the bottom of the gorge. He landed in a huge pile of rubble and refuse, but scrambled to his feet in seconds, running like hell after Phoenix.

Spartan raced back down the main street and saw the elderly rat burger vendor sprawled in front of her little stall, her charcoal grill overturned. The woman struggled up to her knees and pointed into her restaurant. The Scraps who had been lounging there a few minutes before, puffing on cigarettes, were gone.

Spartan burst into the room, running low, his gun out. But the room was empty. The rickety chairs were stacked up in a haphazard pile. Spartan looked up. In the roof of the room was a trapdoor.

"Son of a bitch!" Spartan jumped and hauled himself up into the gap, staring into the blackness. Running straight up into the rock was a wide steel-walled shaft split by a long steel cable. Phoenix was clambering up the line with easy dexterity.

Spartan dropped back down into the restaurant. Lenina Huxley was waiting for him, panting and red-cheeked. She was both elated and horrified by the explosion of violence.

"What's going on?" she asked.

"This is an elevator," said Spartan. "This whole room is a freight elevator, the shaft goes straight up to the surface."

Spartan stripped some old tattered posters from the wall, revealing a control panel and the old up-down handle.

Huxley grinned. "Going up?"

"Yeah," said Spartan. Then he thought. "No. Wait." He grinned devilishly. "Momentito, Señorita Huxley." He dashed down the main street of the Wasteland, running back toward the workshop.

"Now what?" said Huxley, shaking her head.

20

One of the few pleasures shared by people of San Angeles 2032 and the people of Los Angeles in the twentieth century was the simple joy of shopping for a new car. There was only one car manufacturer left in the brave new world—the mega-corporation General Electric Motors—and the main showroom was in Century City.

On any given day San Angelenos could be found wandering around the vast dealership admiring the 2033 models that had just been delivered to the distributor.

There was the budget Serenity, the sporty Composure GT, a minivan aimed at families and marketed under the name Homebody; and for the more affluent there was a luxury car, a sleek, roomy automobile called the Equanimity. Not one of these automobiles did over fifty-five miles an hour—and why should they? After all, driving at fifty-*six* miles an hour would constitute an offense against the law.

As the shoppers wandered among the shiny new automobiles, the gleaming tile floor suddenly began to tremble and there was a rumbling in the air. The people exchanged worried glances and glanced at the floor.

"But . . . but," stammered one man, "earthquakes have been outlawed."

Then the floor began to quiver, and a spiderweb of cracks snaked across it, tiles flipping up like fish out of water. The roaring got louder, and suddenly the freight elevator burst through the pavement like a whale breaking the surface, tossing aside a bright new Composure GT. The would-be car buyers stared for a moment—then ran screaming for the exits.

From inside the elevator cab came the roaring of a powerful engine, then, a second later, the Oldsmobile blasted through the wall and skidded across the shiny floor and stopped just shy of the big plate glass windows enclosing the dealership.

Spartan was at the wheel, Lenina Huxley crouched in the passenger seat.

"Now what?" she asked, yet again.

Spartan grinned. "Vaya con dios!"

He dropped the Cutlass into gear, and the car blasted straight through the glass in a shower of crystal shards, zoomed across the green lawn in front of the dealership, and out onto the highway.

One of the mystified and terrified car buyers watched it go, and frightened though he was, he did recognize a great car when he saw one.

The throaty roar of the Olds awoke some deep, long-dormant atavistic impulse in the West Coast American male—the innate love of powerful, wasteful transportation. Never mind the sedate, polite, *boring* General Electric Motors, Serenity, Composure, Homebody, or Equanimity.

"I want one of *those*," he said, his eyes bright with automotive lust.

Simon Phoenix emerged from the lower depths tired, greasy, and dripping with sweat—but strangely exhilarated. The battle underground had gotten his blood pumping, and he was more hopped-up and crazy than he had ever been. He had tasted blood, and he wanted more . . . Specifically, he wanted the taste of John Spartan's blood. And, like a figure in a bad dream, he scuttled off into the night in search of his prey.

Zachary Lamb had found the entrance to the Wasteland that John Spartan had used, the wrenched open sewer duct at the corner of Wilshire and Santa Monica Boulevard. For some time now he had been standing watch over it, waiting for his old friend to reemerge from the depths.

He had no doubt that Spartan was down there— particularly when he heard the explosions reverberating through the netherworld. That could only mean one thing. Zach Lamb looked concerned and pleased at the same time—the peace officer of San Angeles was disturbed that the public order was being interfered with; the old LAPD cop that lurked somewhere in his soul was elated that things were going back to "normal."

"Yeah," he said delightedly. "John Spartan, the Demolition Man is back."

From behind him Simon Phoenix spoke. His words were as cold as ice. "So am I, rookie."

Zach Lamb whipped around and found himself looking down the barrel of an old Colt twenty-two caliber handgun. Phoenix was festooned with the weapons he had stolen from the museum the day before and had stashed somewhere in the neighborhood.

Far our in the night, from the direction of Century City, they could hear the powerful roar of the Olds. It was getting closer with the passage of every second.

"You haven't got a chance, Phoenix," said Lamb, hoping to stay alive long enough until Spartan arrived.

But it was not to be.

"Neither have you," said Phoenix. He fired six times, each bullet blasting into Zach Lamb's body.

He toppled to the ground, a bloody heap, and tried to crawl a few inches, but his strength was ebbing away, flowing out of him with his blood.

Phoenix stood over the dying man, his pistol aimed for the final shot, the kill shot to the head.

"Phoenix," Zach Lamb gasped painfully. "You're still . . . one ugly sonofabitch."

Phoenix smiled. "You shouldn't have said that—now I'm going to have to kill you . . ." Then he laughed his crazy laugh. "Ah damn! I forgot. I already did!"

He fired the final shot, the bullet smashing into Lamb's brain. Then he ran for the fallen man's police car and zoomed out into the night.

Fifteen or twenty seconds later the Olds screeched to a halt next to Zachary Lamb's lifeless body, Spartan leaping from the car even before it stopped moving.

"Lamb!" John Spartan dropped to his knees next to his fallen friend and held his hand for a moment.

Lenina Huxley stood over the two men. "I empathize with your loss," she said softly.

Then Spartan looked down Santa Monica and saw the taillights of a car rushing away far faster than normal for a sedate San Angeles driver. He laid Zach's body back down on the warm asphalt. There was nothing he could do for Lamb now—except avenge him.

Spartan stood up and ran back to his twentieth-century automotive behemoth. He wrenched the car into gear and floored it, peeling out so fast and furiously that Lenina Huxley felt the g-forces pinning her to her seat.

"John Spartan!" she squeaked. "Be careful!"

"What for?" he snarled, as the Olds zoomed out onto the shiny San Angeles boulevard.

He drove like a man possessed, as if there was nothing on the road—nothing in the world—that could stop him. He muscled the car down the freeway, plowing through the gentle little automobiles of the new world like a bully swaggering through a crowd of schoolgirls. He passed on the left, the right, in the break-down lanes, and on sidewalks. If there wasn't room enough to pass between two cars, he made it.

Spartan left a trail of destruction in his wake as dented and bashed-in cars skidded and slid, careening around the road, piling up a chain of accidents that stretched all the way back to Beverly Hills.

Then he had Phoenix in view. The criminal was driving recklessly as well, but his stolen vehicle—a police-modified version of last year's General Electric Motors Imperturbable-Turbo—did not have anything like the power of the ancient Oldsmobile.

Spartan thrust his left hand out the window and fired, the stream of slugs slamming into the body of Phoenix's car, but failing to stop him or even to slow him down. The angle was all wrong—Spartan couldn't drive and shoot at the same time, not if he wanted to be effective.

"Fuck it," he said, pulling his arm back into the car.

With one hand on the wheel Spartan straight-armed the Beretta and aimed at his own windshield, drawing a bead on the rear of Phoenix's car. He had the wildly fishtailing vehicle in his sights for a split second, and he did not hesitate, firing through the windshield. The glass shattered, showering Spartan and Huxley with tiny nuggets of safety glass.

This time Spartan's shells did a little more damage, blasting out the rear window of the police car, a bullet nicking Phoenix's neck, blood bursting from the wound.

"Shit!" screamed Phoenix. He touched his hand to the injury and felt his own blood, warm and sticky. "Now I'm mad!"

He grabbed a machine pistol from his bag of tricks, half turned in the driver's seat, and fired through the splintered rear window. The vicious little gun chattered, chewing up the front grille of the Oldsmobile and blasting out what little glass remained in the windshield. Quickly emptying the automatic, he tossed it aside and felt for another weapon.

But Spartan had settled down, and his aim was improving. He fired two carefully placed shots at the retreating car and blew out both rear tires. With a scream of shredding rubber and superheated brakes, Phoenix's car swerved wildly out of control, sideswiping a couple of parked cars and taking out a row of parking meters.

"Auto inflate!" he screamed at the sensor mounted in the dash, and instantly the backup tires inflated, throwing the car sideways. Phoenix wrestled the car on track, fighting to put himself back on a straight course.

Spartan thought he had him that time. He pounded the wheel in frustration. "Damn!" He glanced to his right and saw that Lenina Huxley was holding on tight, her eyes wide with fright and excitement.

"Take over!" Spartan yelled over the roar of the engine. "Take the wheel."

"What! You must be out of your—"

Spartan didn't have time to argue. He reached over and grabbed the young woman by the shoulder and hauled her out of her seat and into his lap. Then he pushed himself up and out through the shattered windshield, Lenina dropping down into the seat he had just vacated.

Huxley barely managed to hold onto the steering wheel as the car lurched suddenly to the right.

"Drive," ordered Spartan. "Keep it fast and steady."

"So what, I just push one of these pedals . . .?"

Huxley was holding the wheel, but wasn't looking where she was going. She was peering down at her feet, trying to guess which pedal was the brake, which was the accelerator, and which was the clutch.

She shrugged her shoulders and guessed. She hit the gas, pushing it all the way to the floor. The engine screamed, and the whole car bounded forward, burning rubber as the heavy machine rocketed ahead.

Spartan wasn't ready for the lurch, and he was thrown back, hanging on with one hand curled around the jagged lip of the ruined windshield.

He lay on his stomach on the buckling roof and fired at Phoenix's car. The full clip seemed to perforate the vehicle's body, punching a dozen holes in the metal and swatting the side mirrors off the doors. Phoenix wove back and forth like a fighter pilot taking evasive action, trying to shake off a bandit on his tail.

He glanced into his rearview mirror. The chewed front of the Olds was getting bigger and bigger as the car bore down on him, looking as if it would steamroller right over the flimsy police cruiser.

"Time to get outta here," he said. What he really needed was more speed—and that meant persuading the internal speed governor on the automobile that he needed to go faster.

"Computer!" Phoenix barked. "Velocity control override!"

The computer wasn't going to be swayed so easily. "State nature of the emergency," the happy female voice asked.

"Arson," yelled Phoenix. The car sped up a little, gaining a few miles an hour. It wasn't enough.

"Armed robbery!"

Grudgingly, the override doled out a tiny bit more acceleration.

Phoenix was frantic now, the Olds almost on him. "No! it's better than armed robbery—"

The car slowed down.

"*Worse!*" Phoenix corrected himself. "Worse than armed robbery. No, it's murder. An entire family is being robbed in a burning building, and they're all getting killed! The whole family. Even the dog!"

That was enough to alarm even an unflappable computer. The machine took the speed governor off completely and the car rocketed away.

Watching the speed of the police car pick up dramatically, Lenina Huxley knew in a heartbeat what Phoenix had managed to do.

"He's accessed velocity override!"

"Don't worry about it," Spartan yelled back. "Just punch it!"

"Excuse me?" screamed Lenina Huxley.

"Push the pedal down as hard as you can," ordered Spartan. "Now!"

Lenina Huxley was pretty sure she had done that already, but she found a little more give in the accelerator, and the car zoomed ahead, throwing Spartan forward onto the hot hood.

"Whoa! Whoa!" he screamed. "Slow down! Slow *down!*"

But it was too late. Lenina was hardly in control of the car as it was; slowing down, down shifting and backing off was far beyond her skills.

A second later the nose of the Olds rammed into the rear of the police cruiser, the force of impact catapulting Spartan onto the trunk. He fell heavily, denting the metal, and the Beretta flew out of his hand and soared into the night, clattering onto the roadway.

"Great," said Spartan. "Just terrific."

Phoenix could see that Spartan was hanging on— and he didn't like that. He shoved a MAC 10 out of the side window and fired, a line of bullets stitching across the rear quarter of the car. Spartan dove for the gun and smashed Phoenix's hand against the metal, then wrenched the weapon away. But just as he was ready to fire, Phoenix screamed loudly.

"Open doors! Emergency! Emergency!"

The gullwing doors of the police cruiser flipped open, throwing Spartan aside, tossing him up onto the roof of the vehicle. The gun was bashed from his hands, and he fell flat to the metal.

Spartan was spread-eagle on the roof of the police car, his nails frantically digging into the paint finish, trying to find any kind of handhold. But the sleek aerodynamics of the car were almost perfect, and the wind rushing at him at more than a hundred miles an hour was blowing him backward.

The terrible fall would probably kill him—but it didn't. Lenina was right there, right behind the cruiser, and she would probably run him over. It woud be an accident, and Lenina would feel bad— but Spartan would still be just as dead.

Using all the strength he possessed, Spartan launched himself forward and wrapped one hand around the edge of one of the still open doors. He edged forward and jammed his shoulder between the door and the frame.

"Close doors!" ordered Phoenix.

The right door slammed shut, while the left crushed against Spartan's shoulder. He breathed deep and pushed back. The hydraulic mechanism whined in protest and Spartan growled.

For a few seconds it was man against machine, each trying to destroy the other. But Spartan had more riding on the outcome—he could not afford to lose. With a burst of superhuman effort he wrenched the closing mechanism clean out of the door and then, for good measure, tore the door from its hinges, tossing the sheet metal into the street.

Then Spartan slipped around the side and dropped straight into the car, throwing himself at Phoenix, punching him square in the head.

Phoenix slammed into the side of the vehicle, bounced off the door and came back at Spartan with everything he had, triple-punching his enemy in the chest. The cryo-rehab was still pulsing through Phoenix's veins, and that plus the adrenaline surge he always got with pure violence made him stronger than John Spartan.

The car was on auto-drive, so Phoenix was free to jump from the controls on Spartan. He shoved him out of the open door, grabbing him by the throat and thrusting his head out over the curb. They were rushing toward a fire hydrant, a few hundred pounds of cold pig iron, planted on the sidewalk. The pile of ungiving steel and Spartan's head were definitely on a collision course. If they hit, it would not be pretty.

"You're dead, Spartan."

Spartan grabbed Phoenix by the shoulders. "Speak for yourself."

He hurled Phoenix over his head, catapulting him out of the car, throwing the maniac into the night. Spartan hauled himself into the car, missing the hydrant by inches.

But there was a new obstacle to worry about. The car was doing better than a hundred and forty miles an hour—and it was aimed directly at the mammoth San Angeles Police Department headquarters building.

Doubtless there was some kind of built-in anticollision system in the car, but Spartan didn't have a clue how to activate it. Better to do things the old-fashioned way.

"Self-drive now!" screamed Spartan, and the steering wheel popped out of the dash. He grabbed and wrenched, but it was too late. The car hit the curb and vaulted into the night sky, going completely airborne. As it smashed into the glass wall of the police building, Spartan got the feeling he had suddenly driven into a blizzard.

Nozzles popped from the floor of the station, spewing great geysers of thick, heavy foam. The showers of froth encased the car, filled it, and slowed it down, as if Spartan had driven into a giant vat of marshmallows.

It was a curiously gentle end to such a wild ride—Spartan wasn't sorry it was over.

21

John Spartan struggled out of the cloud of white foam, hacking and coughing, wiping the stuff from his face. Lenina Huxley knew enough about driving a twentieth-century muscle car to bring it to a halt. She jumped out of the car and ran over to the wrecked police cruiser.

"I thought your life force had been prematurely terminated," she said breathlessly.

Spartan was still rubbing the foam from his face and tattered uniform. "Yeah, I thought I was screwed this time, too." He whipped his hands toward the ground, throwing off foam. "What is this stuff?"

"Securofoam," said Lenina Huxley. "Many public buildings are protected by it."

"I hate it," said Spartan.

Despite her wild ride Lenina Huxley was still a member of the SAPD. "Look at you," she said shaking her head. "You're a shambles!"

"Don't worry about my uniform," he said. "I'll just knit myself a new one."

Chief Earle was bearing down on them. He was red in the face and his eyes bulged. "John Spartan!" he screeched. "You . . . you caveman! You are under arrest. You are to be returned to the Cryo-Penitentiary forthwith!"

Spartan all but ignored the man. "Yeah, I heard about that. Look, we'll talk later, okay?" He walked away from the police chief and started searching through the wreckage and foam.

"What are you doing?" asked Huxley.

"I need something, anything. A shotgun. A flare gun . . ." But Phoenix's arsenal had vanished. "Damn," he said. Then he looked up. "Holy shit!"

Chief Earle couldn't believe his eyes either. "Stun batons on," he sputtered.

Coming across the green lawns surrounding the police station were a hoard of Scraps, Edgar Friendly in the lead. Spartan's daughter, Katherine, was walking among them. Spartan smiled proudly— he expected no less.

Every man was armed to the teeth—even the rebels carrying the litters bearing the bodies of the dead cryo-cons, killed in the subterranean firefight. Their corpses were draped with torn, dirty sheets, covering their chests and faces.

But strangest of all was the sight of Alfredo Garcia walking with the Scraps as if he belonged with them.

Spartan grinned. "Hey Garcia, you get a bump

on the head and all of a sudden you become Pancho Villa.''

"Who?" asked Garcia.

"Never mind."

"The time has come for us to take a stand," Friendly announced. The other Scraps nodded in agreement.

"That's good," said Spartan. "Real good. But while you're at it, could you loan me a gun. Maybe two guns? Two guns would be better."

Immediately, Scraps stepped forward, offering arms and ammunition from their ample supplies. Gratefully, Spartan strapped on two heavy handguns and crisscrossed his chest with two thick belts of ammunition. Now *he* looked like Pancho Villa . . .

Chief Earle was almost on the verge of tears. Guns always made him feel a little sick. His head spun—Scraps in his police station, guns, destroyed police cars . . . Truly, his world was coming to an end.

"You would use these weapons of mass destruction against the men and women who uphold the law?" Chief Earle asked incredulously.

Friendly smiled thinly. "We would use these weapons to shop for groceries."

Spartan was ignoring this little exchange. Instead, he walked over to the litters and examined the bodies of the dead cryo-cons the Scraps had carried up from the Wasteland.

When he saw their faces, he was stunned.

"Who are these swarthy strangers?" asked Huxley.

"I know these guys," said Spartan. "I arrested them years ago . . . Beppo Collins, the owner of twenty-two murders—at least, those are the ones we know about.''

"And the other?" asked Huxley.

"Kodo Obata," said Spartan, his voice hollow. "I don't even want to tell you what he did." He looked very grim. "And they're out. There were more of them down there . . ." Simon Phoenix didn't seem to care how much trouble he caused. Bringing these guys out of the cryo-pen was like opening Pandora's box. "I never thought I'd see these guys again. Kind of hoping I wouldn't." The fact that Kodo and Beppo were finally dead did not seem to reassure him all that much.

"I once checked," said Lenina Huxley proudly. "Prior to your own cryo-incarceration, forty-five of the two hundred members in the multilife sentence wing of the cryo-prison were your arrests. Quite a record . . ."

"Right now that's not a very reassuring statistic," said Spartan. He couldn't help wondering how many of those forty-five Phoenix had sprung to join him in cutting a violent swath here in the future.

"Hey, Dad," said Katherine, walking up to her father. "Here." She held something out in her hand. "You gave me this once. I think you might need it now."

Katherine opened her hand. Spartan looked down and saw that she was clutching his old Los Angeles Police Department badge. It was dented and tarnished and rusted around the edges, but it remained his personal badge of office.

"Thank you," he said.

Katherine hugged him close. "For what it's

worth, you have a family now," she said through her tears. "So try be careful, okay?"

Spartan nodded. "I will."

Katherine laughed. "No, you won't. Good luck, Dad."

"Thanks kid." He smiled at his daughter gently, looking at her closely. Behind the wrinkles around the eyes and the smudge of dirt on her cheek, he could see the features of his wife. He felt as if thirty-six years of pain were washing away.

Spartan strode over to the smoking Oldsmobile 442 and slipped behind the wheel. Lenina Huxley took her place in the passenger seat.

Chief Earle capered around the car, waving his arms. "You can't leave. You're under arrest! This very concept negates the possibility of your departure."

"Skip it." Turning the key in the ignition, he fired up the 442. Spartan revved the engine. The ground seemed to tremble and the air around the engine got hot.

"Hey, Chief," said Spartan. "Negate this."

Earle turned to Huxley. "Lieutenant! I order you to place this man—"

Lenina cut him off abruptly. "Chief, take this job and shovel it."

Spartan looked at her, wondering if he should correct her. He decided against it.

"Close enough," he said. Then he stomped on the accelerator, and the Olds roared out into the night. There were bad guys out there, and John Spartan was going to find them. And then he was going to kill them.

In the entire history of the city of San Angeles, there had never been a more peculiar gathering in Cocteau's office than the one going on right at that moment. Cocteau was actually delighted to see Simon Phoenix and his outlandishly violent-looking band of killers striding into his office. Associate Bob, who tended to be a bit more timid, was less ecstatic.

"I wasn't counting on this," said Cocteau, "but I must say you have worked out wonderfully, Simon Phoenix. People are terrified of you."

Phoenix shrugged. "So what else is new? People have always been terrified of me."

Cocteau nodded. "Of course, but the good citizens of San Angeles could never have dreamed that a fellow such as yourself ever existed. With your coming they are truly intimidated. Very gratifying—"

"I'll bet," said Phoenix.

"Was Friendly a problem?" Cocteau asked. "Or did you catch him completely off guard?"

Phoenix was toying with the Airweight .38-caliber pistol stuffed into his belt. "Oh, Friendly? We caught him off guard."

Cocteau clapped his hands in joy, imagining the scene—Edgar Friendly suddenly set upon by Simon Phoenix and his crew and the Scraps leader having no clue whatsoever what had hit him.

"That is marvelous work, Simon Phoenix. Absolutely marvelous."

Phoenix shrugged modestly. "Yeah, well, you know how it is, Ray."

"Now," said Cocteau. "Without him we will be able to separate the rest of the Scraps into isolated groups and administer an enzyme injection that will ensure the same IQ, the same needs, the same desire to think only happy thoughts—"

"We will?" said Phoenix. "*We* will?"

"And with the panic you'll create when I unleash you fully, the rest of the population will demand security cameras in every room, even bathrooms!"

"Yeah," said Phoenix, "I've been meaning to ask you. Bathrooms. What is it with those three little seashells? I can't figure out what the hell is going on with those things. I mean, instead of *toilet paper*? What kind of bullshit is that anyway? I mean, it doesn't make sense, Ray. I thought things in the future were supposed to be better."

But Cocteau was not paying attention. He was consumed with a vision of an even better San Angeles. "There will be more alarm systems controlling all kinds of misbehavior. There will be hot lines where people can inform on their neighbors' infractions. I'll have carte blanche to create the perfect society. My society.''

"*Your* society?" said Phoenix. That wasn't how he planned things at all.

"San Angeles will be a beacon of purity with the order of an ant colony and the beauty of a flawless pearl.''

"Yeah," said Phoenix. "Right." He pulled the Airweight revolver from his belt and aimed it at Cocteau's head, his finger resting lightly on the trigger. "You know, Ray, I think you may have made a mistake.''

"A mistake? What mistake?''

"You can't take away people's right to be assholes," he said, looking along the barrel of the gun. "It's un-American." Phoenix tugged on the trigger, but he couldn't pull it. He had forgotten that there was something in him that would not let him kill Cocteau, who continued to smile serenely.

"Come, come, Simon Phoenix. Did you think I would bring you out of cryo-suspension without taking the precaution of programming you to be incapable of doing me physical harm? Please. You underestimate me. Simon Phoenix, you are incapable of killing me. You could never shoot me—not even if your life depended on it.''

"You know . . . ever since I met you, Ray," said Phoenix, shaking a finger at Cocteau, "you've reminded me of someone." He thought for a moment. "Nope. Can't place you.''

Cocteau smiled politely. He really wasn't all that interested in anything Simon Phoenix had to say.

"So, you see, you cannot kill me, Simon Phoenix. So you might as well do my bidding."

Phoenix nodded. "That's right. What can I say? You're right. *I* can't kill you. But *he* can." Simon Phoenix tossed the revolver to the nearest thug. "Do me a favor," he said. "Grease this guy. He's pissing me off."

Fear raced across Cocteau's features as he realized his mistake. He had not, of course, programmed every cryo-con to be allergic to killing the Mayor-Gov.

The goon—it was a mass-murderer named Adam—caught the gun and without hestitation fired, blasting eight shots into Cocteau's chest and head. The Mayor-Gov flew out of his chair and tumbled into the fireplace that decorated his office.

"Somebody put another log on the fire . . ." said Simon Phoenix. He looked at the dead former leader. Then he slapped his knee. "That's it! That's who you remind me of—an evil Mr. Rogers."

"Good one, boss," said Adam.

"No . . . really. That's who he reminds me of. Well, *reminded* me of." He turned to leave the room, then noticed Associate Bob cowering in a corner. "Oooh, who do we have here?"

Associate Bob looked very frightened, but it was plain that he didn't give a damn about the sudden demise of Mayor-Gov Raymond Cocteau. He was worried about his own skin.

"So," said Simon Phoenix. "What shall I do with you, Associate Bob?"

Associate Bob smiled diffidently. "I am an excellent associate, sir. I could work for you."

"Me? I got people who work for me." He pointed

at his four remaining murderous goons. "Why the hell would I need you?"

"Well," said Associate Bob, "Dr. Cocteau had me endocrinologically altered to never wish to be anything but an associate."

"Really?" Simon Phoenix looked over his crew. They were so stupid—and violent—that one or more of them would probably, at some time, get it into his head to challenge Simon Phoenix for leadership of the new San Angeles. He could deal with it if it happened—but it would be a bore to always be watching your ass like that.

"Tell me, Bob," he said. "Just how is it that you never want to be anything more than number two."

"Simple," said Bob. "I believe the slang that would best express it across our chronological gap, sir, would be that he cut my balls off."

"Literally?" asked Phoenix.

Bob nodded. Phoenix laughed and clapped Associate Bob on the shoulder. "Bob," he said, "it's a sign of weakness to cut the balls off the people who work for you. I'm gonna get you a new set."

"Why thank you, sir," said Associate Bob.

"In fact, I'm gonna get a couple extra myself," he said. "Not that I need them. But just for spares, you know?"

Associate Bob nodded, seamlessly transferring his loyalties from one master to another. He was now completely Simon Phoenix's man—and he had to admit that things would probably be a lot more exciting with the new regime than they had been with the old.

"Sir, if I could interrupt . . ."

"Interrupt?" said Phoenix angrily. "Associates don't interrupt, Bob."

"I agree, sir," said Bob. "But I thought you might want to know that the police are here." He pointed through the tall glass windows. The Oldsmobile with Spartan at the wheel and Lenina Huxley riding shotgun pulled up in front of the building.

Phoenix nodded and then turned back to Associate Bob. It looked as though he would need the services of the little guy immediately. "I'm gonna need to defrost more guys, Bob. Lots more guys. Can you do that?"

Associate Bob nodded. "Indubitably. But the computer codes will have to emanate from this office. So we will need a few moments here before fleeing." He sat down at Cocteau's desk and began typing fast on the computer keyboard. As he worked, he leaned over and whispered in Phoenix's ear.

"I might suggest," he said sotto voce, "that you send some of your gentlemen downstairs . . ." He coughed discreetly. "They may be disposable, after all, considering the supply I am ordering for you. Perhaps they could be sent to welcome Mr. Spartan. If they succeed, so much the better. If not, at least they will hinder his progress."

Phoenix nodded and smiled. "I like you, Bob. You have no heart." He turned to his thugs. "Guys, John Spartan is on his way. Go downstairs. Kill him."

The collection of killers nodded. "Kill him over and over," said Adam.

"That's my boy," said Phoenix.

The instant his troops had departed, Phoenix

leaned over the computer terminal watching as Associate Bob typed in the cryo-thaw instructions.

"Now, Bob, I want really evil violent multilifers. I want guys who understand that crimes come in bunches. Not just a sporadic bit of violence or law breaking here and there. I want you to find me some very mean, very stupid lawbreakers, Bob. Got it? Understand?"

"Oh, yes sir, absolutely." said Bob, typing to the specifications of his new boss.

"I want guys who have been on killing sprees before. Men who have crossed state lines with impunity. Do you understand me, Bob?"

Associate Bob didn't even look up from his task. "Perfectly, sir."

Phoenix dropped into a butter smooth leather chair and planted his feet on the desk and watched as Bob continued to order up his homicidal maniac cocktail.

"I'm gonna like running this place," he said happily. "I always wanted a job in administration.

Now . . . all he had to do was get rid of John Spartan. But that would be the fun part.

2 3

The doors of the private elevator belonging to the late Dr. Raymond Cocteau slid open and three Phoenix thugs, Danzig, Elvin, and Francis were lying in ambush. All three opened fire at once, raking the cab with a hundred powerful rounds. Only after they had reduced the elevator to a smoking ruin did the three bother to look inside. It was empty.

None of the three noticed Spartan and Huxley entering the lobby from the stairwell and sneaking away down the long, thickly carpeted corridor.

Spartan couldn't believe that they had managed to get onto the floor so easily. "Old trick," he said, shaking his head.

"Old criminals," said Huxley with a broad grin.

"Don't get cocky," Spartan warned her soberly. "Cocky gets you killed."

"Right."

Suddenly, Spartan tensed like a bird dog, listening for the sounds of heavy footsteps padding down the carpeted hallway, a giant shadow preceding the man.

"Elvin!" shouted Spartan.

Elvin stepped into view. "Yeah?"

"Thought it was you." Spartan fired once, a perfectly aimed shot to the heart. The big goon toppled over, dead in a matter of seconds.

Despite John Spartan's warning, Lenina Huxley was feeling invincible. "Let's go get Phoenix," she said eagerly. "Let's end this now!"

Spartan nodded and ran forward, darting across the lobby and heading for Cocteau's suite of offices. Lenina was right behind him.

Danzig was waiting for them, perched like a gargoyle on the railing of the interior balcony that overlooked the entrance to Associate Bob's work station. The instant Spartan was in range, the big man dropped from his roost like a bird of prey.

Spartan never saw him coming—but he felt him. Danzig slammed down onto Spartan's back, knocking him to the ground and pounding the breath out of him. The bad guy grabbed a handful of hair and slammed Spartan forehead first into the floor, but it was too cushioned to do him much damage.

Spartan flipped and kicked, spearing Danzig in the chest and then falling on him. The two men grappled, fighting in close, rabbit chops and kidney punches flying.

Lenina yanked the stun baton from her belt,

activated it, and moved in, trying to assist her partner. But as Spartan and Danzig twisted and tumbled, she stood uncertainly, afraid to act—she was just as likely to paralyze Spartan as Danzig. She never saw the last killer, Francis, moving in on her.

He slapped away the stun baton, and then one huge dirty hand closed around her neck, lifting her off the floor, choking her as if the big man had converted his entire body into a human gallows. Lenina kicked and clawed, but her puny blows seemed to have no effect whatsoever. Francis smiled evilly as he throttled the life from her body.

Lenina could feel her throat fuse and the dark clouds of unconsciousness beginning to close around her brain. With a jolt she realized that she was just moments away from death. In desperation she reached out and found her hand closing around the handle of Francis's gun. She wrenched it from the holster and before the killer could react, cocked the old revolver and fired.

The bullet slammed straight into Francis's gut, knocking him back against the wall. Lenina picked herself up and holding the gun in both hands, let him have it three more times—one shot to the heart, two to the head just to make sure.

Spartan was just finishing up with Danzig. He elbowed him hard in the ribs, flipped him around, and buried his knee in his back. Vertebrae popped like firecrackers, and he fell to the floor, twitching in his death throes.

Lenina was in a state of shock. She had never fought before; she had certainly never killed. She had hardly even been touched by another human being, never mind by one who was trying to murder her.

"This man has died at my hands," she said shakily. "I have taken all his future from him."

"It was either him or you, Huxley," said Spartan.

Lenina felt the bruises on her neck and remembered with a shudder the sensation of having her throat squeezed shut. "You may have a point there."

"C'mon," said Spartan, racing for the Mayor-Gov's office.

The room was empty—except for the lifeless body of Raymond Cocteau.

Huxley couldn't quite believe that the leader and visionary was dead. "Sic transit Raymond Cocteau," she said. "Oh, John Spartan, civilization as we know it will come to an end. What do we do now?"

"I don't know," Spartan replied. "Put up a statue? Have a parade?"

Spartan was far less affected by the sudden, violent end of the Mayor-Gov. He was peering at the man's computer screen, trying to make sense of the data. "What's this?"

Lenina Huxley checked out the information and paled. "Ooh, this is bad. Very bad."

"What did he do?"

"The cryo-prison has been accessed," said Lenina. "He's about to defrost the entire multilifer wing . . . Most of these people don't like you."

If she expected Spartan's feelings to be hurt, he didn't show it. "Most of them didn't like their mothers." He scanned the names. "How many in total?"

"Eighty."

Spartan winced. "We have to try and stop that," he said, leading the way out of the office. He paused long enough to strip the dead killers of their weaponry, loading himself down with ammunition. Huxley could not take her eyes off the man she had killed.

"Okay," she said, "I wasn't at all pleased to have caused the fatality of that deranged cryo-con, but I understand now that sometimes under particular circumstances that violence is necessary."

Spartan nodded. "That's good, because then you'll understand why I have to do this." He whipped the stun baton from her belt and nailed her with it, zapping her right in the sternum. She was taken completely by surprise.

Lenina Huxley's eyes turned up in her head, and she started to sag. Spartan caught her before she hit the ground and laid her gently in a chair.

The Oldsmobile raced up to the perimeter fence of the Cryo-Penitentiary and screeched to a halt. Spartan checked his weapons, then sat for a moment, watching the forbidding building. There was activity inside. He could hear shouts and the whine of machinery and somewhere within the shrill squeal of an alarm. Simon Phoenix was very busy—and Spartan knew he must have secured some help. Not even he was capable of thawing out eighty cryo-cons without some kind of technical assistance.

Spartan revved the engine. "Send a maniac to catch a maniac." he said, then floored the gas pedal, the big, battered car roaring toward the building.

* * *

The control room of the prison was bustling, Phoenix watching as Associate Bob ordered the technicians to hurry along with the defrosting process. It was dangerous, of course, to do it too fast, but neither Phoenix nor Associate Bob really cared if they lost a cryo-con or two in the process—there were plenty in the ice box.

Twelve ice pods had been removed from the cryogenic floor, and med-techs were scrambling to deice the first three, cutting through them with blue flamed cutting lasers.

Associate Bob looked worried as the perimeter alarm sounded. "There's been a breach of our outer gate," he told Phoenix quickly. "An intruder has entered the cryo-facility, and I feel it's safe to assume it is John Spartan."

"No problem," said Phoenix. The first three cryo-cons, Gunther, Howie, and Jed, were emerging from their ice cells, and they looked a little dopey and unsteady on their feet. Phoenix turned to one of the medical technicians.

"Hey buddy, you got some really wild uppers? Speed, crank, amphetamines? Anything like that?"

"We have pure mega-adrenaline, sir."

"That sounds good," said Phoenix. "Shoot 'em up."

"Yes, sir." The medical technician quickly plunged needles into the dazed killers, and suddenly they became completely awake. Their eyes widened, and they jerked spastically, their brains frying as the drug kicked in.

Phoenix kept it simple. "Hey! Wake up."

"Huh?" said Jed. "What the fuck—"

"Shuttup," ordered Phoenix. "Listen to me.

You've just been defrosted. It's the future. John Spartan is around here someplace.''

"Spartan!" screeched Howie.

"Right," said Phoenix. "You guys, go kill him."

Gunther let out a blood-curdling scream and ran, charging out of the wide double doors in search of John Spartan, his two fellow cryo-cons right behind him.

Spartan was in the lobby of the prison, cautiously making his way into the interior of the building. The entrance hall was deserted and suspiciously quiet, no guard waiting at the reception desk. Hunched and low, Spartan stole forward, his weapon at the ready. If Phoenix had thawed any of his deadly assistants, Spartan's most useful weapon would be surprise.

He didn't think he had been detected, but he failed to notice a tiny sensor that immediately locked onto him. Suddenly, the big vid screen behind the reception desk burst into life, a smiling hologram of Dr. Cocteau appearing on the screen.

"Greetings," he said, beaming. "And be well." Spartan raised his weapon and blasted the screen into a thousand tiny pieces of plastic. "I hate reruns," he growled.

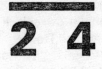

The three cryo-cons came barreling through the doors, straight at Spartan. The first one, Gunther, didn't get very far. Spartan shot him dead, a single shot to the forehead. But before he could fire again, the other two were on him.

Jed pummeled Spartan, smashing him in the ribs and chest while Howie tried to wrest the gun from his hand. Spartan raised his arm, as if signaling keep away, and swung on Jed who was beginning to annoy him. His fist thumped into the man's jaw, and Jed's mouth appeared to collapse as his teeth crunched into dozens of tiny particles. Jed sagged to the floor.

Now it was Howie's turn. The cryo-con hadn't stopped tussling for the gun, and Spartan had had just about enough. He held the weapon out.

"Fine. Here. Take it."

Howie snatched the gun and still in shock and cranked up on mega-adrenaline, fumbled with the unfamiliar hardware for a moment, trying to get his befuddled brain to figure out what to do next.

He never got a chance to solve the simple equation: gun + shoot = death. Spartan reached out with both hands and broke the man's neck.

Now Jed was back. He jumped from behind, his forearms locking around Spartan's neck. Spartan squat-pressed down with the three-hundred-pound thug on his back, grabbed the gun out of Howie's stiffening fingers, and angled the weapon over his shoulder.

"Get off my back," said Spartan. He fired three times, and Jed slid to the floor.

Spartan didn't hang around. He burst through the double doors and ran into the heart of the building. The multilifer wing was unoccupied, but empty cryo-pods were strewn everywhere. Spartan didn't bother to count them, but the news was bad. Phoenix had managed to spring a lot of very bad guys, and they had probably fanned throughout the entire building.

Then Phoenix's voice echoed in the twilit chamber. "Don't you understand the meaning of give up?"

Spartan dove and rolled, looking for the source of the voice. It was coming from above him, somewhere in the shadow-wrapped rafters of the room.

"You're too late, Spartan," Phoenix yelled. "I've got three more batches in the oven."

Then he saw him, standing on a cryo-pod fifteen or twenty feet up. Associate Bob was at his new master's side. Spartan fired, but the bullet went wide, howling off into the darkness.

Phoenix unslung a machine pistol and ripped off an entire clip of nine-millimeter slugs. Suddenly the entire room seemed to be alive with bullets. Freezer pipes burst like grenades, spewing subzero Freon gas. The temperature began dropping rapidly.

Associate Bob figured he had seen enough, and he started to slink away.

"Where the fuck are you going?" Phoenix demanded.

"I wish you good luck, sir," Bob said, his voice aching with sincerity. "But this is an activity that really does require a set of testicles."

Phoenix could see the reason in that. "True enough, Bob. See you after the show. Be well." Phoenix dropped from his perch, slipping down to the cryo-pod floor. Ice was forming on every surface.

Spartan rolled out of the cloud of freezing gas and threw himself into a thicket of machinery. Everything was coated with supercooled ice, and footing was becoming treacherous.

Phoenix saw Spartan first, drawing a bead on him with the machine pistol and strafing the entire area. The hail of bullets should have cut Spartan down, but Phoenix couldn't hold his weapon steady. The powerful kick from the gun just pushed him back, slipping and sliding on the ice.

Spartan whipped around and fired in the direction of the stream of bullets, but he, too, was driven back by the recoil of his heavy handgun. He braced himself against a steel bulkhead and fired again, only to be answered with another blast of withering fire from Phoenix's machine pistol.

Slipping and sliding, Spartan did his best to lunge for cover, skidding down a flight of iron steps and hitting the lower level of the main cryo-floor. Phoenix probably had a clear shot at him, but he didn't fire.

Cautiously, Spartan got to his feet—only to be body-slammed as a mechanical claw dropped from the ceiling. Both of his guns clattered off, and he leaped for them, but they slithered out of his grasp.

The claw closed around his body, and Spartan could hear Phoenix's insane cackle as the crane hoisted him into the air, dragging him upward toward a cloud of freezing gas.

In an instant ice particles formed on Spartan's clothing, and his skin burned from the intense cold. He struggled in the steel grip, the ice on his body crackling like glass—and reforming in a matter of seconds.

Phoenix was right below him, staring up and watching with excitement as Spartan began to freeze to death before his very eyes. "This is better than shooting!" he screamed. "A lot more entertaining!"

Spartan had no intention of amusing anyone with his death. He reached for the freezing pipe and bent it downward, showering Phoenix with a blast of the supercold vapor. Now it was his turn. He was frozen in place, the ice forming on his clothes like cold armor.

"No way!" Phoenix screamed. He writhed violently, shattering his suit of ice. He roared and broke free, retreating from the gust of supercooled mist.

Spartan let go of the pipe and squirmed out of the claw, dropping to the cold floor. He slid and stumbled on the slick surface and slammed straight into an empty cryo-pod, hitting it hard.

The giant disc shot across the smooth floor, a five-hundred-pound hockey puck—aimed straight at Phoenix. The master bad guy dove to avoid the projectile, throwing himself clear a second before the pod slammed into the steel wall of the room.

"No point in fighting the elements," said Spartan. He lunged forward, sliding along in the path of the pod. It took him three-quarters of a second to skate across the floor, and he ended his little ride with a vicious right hook into Phoenix's surprised face. After all Spartan had been through in the last twenty-four hours, connecting with the punch felt good, deeply satisfying, in fact.

Phoenix slipped backward from the force of the blow and cracked his head on a jungle of pipe. But he was up in a second and laughing. "Hey! Good shot, Spartan!"

Neither man had cracked under the strain yet, but the fabric of the prison itself was not bearing up too well. Lights popped in the cold, pipes burst all over the place, and the machinery screamed and groaned as the intense cold twisted and shattered the metal.

Spartan dove onto Phoenix and landed a horrific blow in his face, all but driving his nose and eye sockets through the back of his skull. Spartan cut himself on exposed bone; the blood spurted from the wound, but almost instantly the gore froze, sealing the wound.

The two men fell onto a tool cart, sending utensils scattering across the slick floor. Spartan grabbed for the most vicious weapon he could find, a fifty-pound lug wrench, a great hunk of old-fashioned heavy iron.

Phoenix went for a more high-tech approach, grabbing a sleek black steel MTL cutting laser. He fired it up and pumped the power up to high, and a thirty-foot spray of bright magnesium thermite light, white hot, swept through the intense cold. Steam formed in the air, and the supercooled metal buckled and snapped.

Suddenly, all of the ice in the room began to melt, boiling away in hot clouds of condensation.

Spartan had nowhere to run, and he was armed with nothing more than his big iron club. Caveman meets the technology of the twenty-first century . . .

All he could do was duck down behind an empty cryo-pod and try to avoid the deadly laser beam long enough to try and turn this horrible situation around.

Spartan peered over the edge of the cryo-pod and watched as the MTL beam swept across the room like a lethal searchlight, melting and burning everything in its path.

Then he looked down into the pod itself. Lying under the bell jar was the white cryo-chip contained in the vacuum urn, the heart of the cryo-freezing system. Spartan grabbed the vial and heaved himself up into the support grid above the pod.

"Coming to get you, Spartan," screamed Phoenix. "Come out, come out, wherever you are . . ."

Spartan hurled the vial at Phoenix's feet, the glass shattering and the white freezing chip rolling free. He hurled himself after the chip, flying over Phoenix's head and dodging the death ray. Spartan landed behind Phoenix and came back at him with a murderous elbow in the kidney. Phoenix doubled over and dropped the MTL laser.

Phoenix whipped around and smacked Spartan hard, mashing a nerve center in the side of Spartan's neck. Suddenly, everything went numb, but he fought back, punching left, right, and left again. Phoenix coughed blood and spat, staggering back a few steps.

The water gathering around the freeze chip was beginning to solidify, and as Phoenix put his boot in the puddle, it froze, seizing his foot.

"Hey!" He looked down and saw that he was rooted fast to the spot, the ice gathering around him. Then the cold started traveling up his legs. He felt his legs freeze rock solid, then his chest and shoulders. The ice raced up his neck and into his head and hair.

He worked his mouth, trying to scream his way out of his frozen veneer, desperately trying to pull his hardened arms away from his body. But he was stuck, frozen stiff and standing straight up. His eyes grew wide as he watched Spartan—his punch seemed to start at the floor, racing up toward Phoenix's chin, his big fist traveling like a bullet.

Spartan hit Phoenix with everything he had, his full body weight behind the blow. His fist smacked into Phoenix's chin. The impact of the blow meeting the frozen face of the maniac snapped Phoenix's head right off his neck—like a flower whipped off its stalk.

Phoenix's head hit the polished steel floor and bounced with a clang, rolling away into a corner like a loose ball bearing.

Spartan looked around him. The building had gone from supercold to superhot and back again. It was more than the structure could stand. Beams were crashing down from the ceiling, and static and sparks were crackling and flashing all over the chamber. Spartan stooped and picked up the MTL laser.

"I think it's time to go . . ."

25

Using the laser like a high-tech machete, John Spartan sliced and diced his way out of the Cryo-Penitentiary, chopping his way through the falling, burning debris. Everywhere the laser touched, metal sparked and buckled—the building literally collapsing around him.

He stalked through the burning reception area and out of the front door, the cold night air hitting him in the face like a punch. Spartan turned and looked at the burning building. If any cryo-cons remained alive within, they wouldn't be for long. Just to help the fire along, he upped the power on the MTL laser and reached back, throwing the weapon deep into the inferno. A second later the night was split by a massive explosion, and the Cryo-Penitentiary started collapsing in on itself, exploding, contracting, a fiery ruin, tumbling down like a house of cards.

A great crowd had gathered at the main gate of the prison—policemen, Scraps, and even ordinary citizens who had dared to break curfew to see what on earth could possibly be happening at the Cryo-Penitentiary.

The Scraps looked delighted as the prison imploded, but Chief Earle and his police force—except for Garcia and Huxley—looked horrified.

Earle stumbled forward as Spartan walked toward the throng. The Chief was in shock, but he did manage to find his tongue and stammer out a question. "You have apprehended the villain who led to the murder of our beloved Mayor-Gov Dr. Raymond Cocteau?"

Spartan looked over his shoulder at the burning, exploding prison. "I don't think 'apprehended' is the word." He jerked a thumb at the inferno. "He's in there with what's left of the cryo-cons and the prison. Cocteau is dead and so are his bastard creations."

"Good riddance to both," said Edgar Friendly.

Earle looked as if he was about to break down and sob. He clutched his cheeks and shook his head. "What will we do?" he wailed. "How will we live?"

"That's easy," said Spartan. "You'll think for yourselves. You'll make decisions. Some will be right and some will be wrong. And you'll live with it. 'Cause that's what life is really like."

He smiled at Chief Earle. "You'll get a little dirty . . ." Then he clapped Friendly on the shoulder, grabbing a handful of grimy shirt. "And you'll get a little clean. You'll figure it out."

Associate Bob was the San Angeleno most used to adapting to change. After all, he had changed sides twice in the last two hours. He looked over the crowd and realized that Chief Earle was a spent force, definitely out of business. Edgar Friendly was plainly the new force in town.

"Greetings and salutations, Edgar Friendly," he said, stepping forward. "I am Associate Bob. May I say that your underground revolutionary movement was one of passion and poetry. I look forward to assisting you in the creation of a more human, less anal San Angeles."

"Los Angeles," Edgar Friendly corrected him. "That's Los Angeles, you dickless wonder."

But Associate Bob refused to be put off. "Almost right," he said with a smile.

Katherine was as deadpan as her father. "You okay?" she asked.

Spartan was broken and bruised, his knuckles skinned and his clothes in tatters. But he was alive. He hugged his daughter. "I'm okay, very okay. I was serious about hearing everything about you. Everything I missed."

"That's forty years' worth of material."

Spartan grinned. "We'll start with kindergarten."

Katherine kissed him on the cheek. "All right, come by for dinner." She looked at the burning prison. "And I think I better do the cooking."

Lenina Huxley studied the father and daughter closely, paying careful attention to their affectionate actions. She kind of liked what she saw.

"So that's it? That's the whole kissing thing. What was Cocteau so worried about?"

"Not quite," said Spartan. He grabbed her and pulled her in, laying a real kiss on her, a genuine, long, hard, tongue twister. Lenina pulled back and came up gasping for air, her eyes bright and shiny.

"Oh, my." she said breathlessly. "Is the rest of fluid transfer activities like this?"

"Better," said Spartan dryly.

"Better! Oh, *my*!" She dove in for another kiss. This time she was the aggressor, locking her lips on his and kissing him for all she was worth.

This time Spartan pulled back. "How am I going to live in this place?"

Lenina Huxley laughed. "How is this place going to live with you? John Spartan, you're going to have to take things one detail at a time."

"One detail at a time?" he said. "Okay. Detail number one: How does that damn three seashells thing work. You know, in the bathrooms . . ."

"Oh, that." Lenina stood on tiptoe and whispered something in his ear.

Spartan's face brightened and his jaw dropped. "No kidding!" he said. "That's amazing! Much better than toilet paper!"

"See," she said, taking his arm. "The future works."

SIGNET

Published or forthcoming

BLOOD ORANGE

Sam Llewellyn

Whether it's Force Eight or financial ruin, ocean racers always sail close to the wind. Yet the wave of bankruptcies and lethal accidents hitting Pulteney is no freak, but a manmade maelstrom of violent extortion and multinational fraud.

Still, when Orange Cars sponsors him for the perilous but lucrative Round the Isles race, James Dixon's problems should be over. Not just beginning . . .

'Sam Llewellyn sends the salt spray flying'
– *Sunday Express*

Published or forthcoming

SIGNET

BASIC INSTINCT

Richard Osborne

A brutal murder.

A brilliant killer.

A cop who can't resist the danger.

When San Francisco detective Nick Curran begins investigating the mysterious and vicious murder of a rock star, he finds himself in a shadowy world where deceit and seduction often go hand in hand. Nick can't stay away from his number one suspect − stunning and uninhibited Catherine Tramell − a novelist whose shocking fiction mirrors the murder down to the smallest, bloodiest detail.

Entangled in love and murder, Nick is headed for trouble, with only his basic instinct for survival to keep him from making a fatal mistake . . .

SIGNET

Published or forthcoming

THE FEATHER MEN
Ranulph Fiennes

In the years between 1977 and 1990, a group of hired assassins known as the Clinic tracked down and killed four British soldiers, one at a time. Two of the victims were ex-SAS. All four had fought in the Arabian desert.

The Feather Men were recruited to hunt the Clinic. Without their intervention more soldiers would have died. At the end of their operation they asked Ranulph Fiennes, one of the world's best-known explorers and himself a former SAS officer, to tell their extraordinary story . . .

The Feather Men is the first account of a secret group with SAS connections – still unacknowledged by the Establishment – who set out to achieve their own form of justice. And how, in September 1990, they finally got their result . . .

SIGNET

Published or forthcoming

THE BOYS FROM BRAZIL

Ira Levin

In a Japanese restaurant in São Paulo, Brazil, six elderly men gather for a reunion dinner. After their meal they admire an engraved cigarette case owned by one of them. Then they are given their instructions.

The man with the cigarette case is Josef Mengele, former Nazi doctor, the instructions a timetable for the assassination of ninety-four insignificant civil servants – men whose deaths would trigger the final victory of the Fourth Reich . . .

'There is no way to stop once you've started' – *Newsweek*

SIGNET

Published or forthcoming

Twilight

Peter James

To those who saw Sally Donaldson's tortured face, it was clear that she had met an unnatural death. A single tragic accident? Or the unthinkable – an experiment gone hideously wrong . . . ?

With the permission of the East Sussex coroner, Sally's body was disinterred from St Anne's Church graveyard. No one was prepared for the horror when the coffin lid was opened.

The authorities begin a bizarre and sinister cover-up. Every witness is sworn to secrecy. But reporter Kate Hemingway refuses to forget. Her investigations into the story are blocked at every turn, until she discovers the research of a brilliant anaesthetist, documenting his lifelong obsession – to prove life after death.

'James certainly knows how to punch across a spine-chilling thrill' – *Evening Standard*

'Authoritative supernatural thriller . . . well-researched, chillingly executed and eminently readable' – *Sunday Times*

SIGNET

Published or forthcoming

Ira Levin
author of *Rosemary's Baby*

Thirteen hundred Madison Avenue, an elegant 'sliver' building, soars high and narrow over Manhattan's smart Upper East Side. Kay Norris, a successful single woman, moves on to the twentieth floor of the building, high on hopes of a fresh start and the glorious Indian summer outside. But she doesn't know that someone is listening to her. Someone is *watching* her.

'Levin really knows how to touch the nerve ends' – *Evening Standard*

'*Sliver* is the ultimate *fin de siècle* horror novel, a fiendish goodbye-wave to trendy urban living ... Ira Levin has created the apartment dweller's worst nightmare' – Stephen King